From the prize-winning author
of the recent and highly successful collection,
THE GODDESS AND OTHER WOMEN,
comes a new book of stories that shows still a
different facet of Miss Oates's incredible
talent: another milieu, characters quite different from those she has drawn so magnifi-
cently in her previous work. Although Miss
Oates has never been to Portugal, she cap-
tures the atmosphere of persons and places
precisely, writing of a world she has never
known but that she sees almost clair-
voyantly. *THE POISONED KISS AND
OTHER STORIES FROM THE PORTU-
GUESE*, from whatever level of consciousness they are written, bear not so much
the stamp of earlier Oates work as they do
a new dimension of their author's art.

THE POISONED KISS

and Other Stories

from the Portuguese

Fernandes / Joyce Carol Oates

A FAWCETT CREST BOOK

Fawcett Publications, Inc., Greenwich, Connecticut

ACKNOWLEDGMENTS: These stories originally appeared in the following magazines: *Carolina Quarterly, Chelsea, December, Harper's Bazaar, The Literary Review, The Massachusetts Review, Partisan Review, Prism International, Southwest Review, Transatlantic Review, Aspen Leaves, The Yale Review,* and *Sparrow.* I am grateful to the editors for permission to reprint.

THE POISONED KISS
and other stories from the Portuguese

THIS BOOK CONTAINS THE COMPLETE TEXT OF THE ORIGINAL HARDCOVER EDITION.

A Fawcett Crest Book reprinted by arrangement with Vanguard Press

ISBN: 0-449-23299-9

Printed in Canada

10 9 8 7 6 5 4 3 2 1

for Marjorie Bitker

... ¡Oh noche, que guiaste,
Oh noche amable más que el alborada:
Oh noche, que juntaste
Amado con amada,
Amada en el Amado transformada!*

     —St. John of the Cross

*. . Oh night that was my guide!
Oh darkness dearer than the morning's pride,
Oh night that joined the lover
To the beloved bride
Transfiguring them each into the other!

(translated by Roy Campbell, in St. John of the Cross, Poems 1960)

Contents

Note

The tales in this collection are translated from an imaginary work, *Azulejos*, by an imaginary author, Fernandes de Briao. To the best of my knowledge he has no existence and has never existed, though without his very real guidance I would not have had access to the mystical "Portugal" of the stories—nor would I have been compelled to recognize the authority of a world-view quite antithetical to my own.

Our Lady of the Easy
Death of Alferce

❦

. . . the warm glimmering shadows like breaths and the whispering beneath me, the whispering, my glazed eyes darker than the shadows ever get . . . I am adored, and I hold the Child in the crook of my right arm . . . his sweet face stares out across the bent heads to the heavy closed doors . . . beyond their carvings the square, the fountain, the roadway . . . the orchards of fig and apricot . . . the hollow sound of the windmills, the *clunking, clunking* of the gourds across the miles . . . golden, golden fields. . . . Green that deepens with rain every spring; the pastures brimming with sunlight and burning and the rotting of wood and the creaking of the carts, the liquid odor of the manure on the wind. . . . *Blessed art Thou amongst women.* . . . Whispering to me, muttering to me, only me. Small candles beneath me in cups of red glass, transparent red glass. The swaying of flames. Breaths. In the crook of my right arm I hold the Child for them to adore: but I have not gazed upon his sweet face for centuries. Staring out at the bent heads, the bent shoulders . . . the shadowy pews where women pray to me. . . . I see their thin white hands, their massive sunburned hands, their fingers, the dip of their brows and noses, the movement of their lips . . . eyes lowered with love, with awe, panting to get inside me across the distance of a few yards. . . . I am adored; a bright tinsel crown has been placed carefully around my wooden crown, which has become dull, and in the cavity of my left thumb and forefinger they have placed a large bouquet of plastic lilies of the valley . . . stark white against the dusty blue of my cloak. . . . Of course the rains, the burning sun, the windmills' arms and shadows, and of course the Child in my arms, the singing of the priest; I am adored, I sleep and wake to my own adoration, my eyes fix themselves upon a solitary man at the back of the church, his hair frizzy from the warm dampness, shoulders scrawny, humped, eyes black across the distance, staring, staring. . . . Love, he is loving me, adoring me, I feel his love and it is a surprise to me, this trembling hot love . . . I yearn to step down from this wooden platform and back away from him, from that look; my long black shiny eyebrows strain to raise themselves in surprise . . . my lips, which are firm and pursed, painted a fleshly pink many years ago and very bright against my face of dull gold, my lips yearn to open and cry out in surprise, in torment. . . . Endless showers fall behind this man, and roads that lead off straight into the sky, the air filled with the creaking of carts, centuries of carts, golden fields broken with rain; the man stares at me through his tumult and I would raise the Child to him, to shield my own face, but I cannot move. I have not looked upon the Child's face for centuries. I know that it is broad as a man's face, painted the same dull golden yellow as my own face, broad as if swollen, and the Child's body is too angular and narrow at the torso and hips for an infant, and his arms are too long, out of proportion, not like the soft plump shapeless babies brought to me for my blessing. Yet the man is staring at us and a film seems to pass over his face, his features shrink inward with desire; there are fences of prickly pear and straight roads rushing across the land and into the sky behind him and yet he kneels there, a man, a solitary man, fixed and staring. . . . He

staggers to his feet. He is whispering something.
. . . *blessed art Thou amongst women*. . . . He
is loving me, I feel his love stirring in him, his
eyes film over with the panicked rage of his love,
he stumbles against something and rights himself
and continues toward me like a sleepwalker . . .
and now I see the pale sweat of his forehead and
the lines of his face, which are too sharp for such
a young man, for he is only a boy, he is not even
a man, and the Child in the crook of my arm
stares down upon him and would free his arm
from mine to ward this boy away, but my fingers
are glued fast to his and we have not moved
apart for centuries, my fingers hold the Child's
small squarish hand firm. . . . How fierce the
boy's love for me!—how terrible his sorrow! . . .
A searing at the edge of my eye . . . something
is happening . . . out of my wide, blank eye
something is moving, forcing itself, squeezing out
. . . I would bring my hand up to my face to
hide it, but I cannot move, and I cannot turn
aside because my feet are glued to this platform
and my robes are fixed, fixed like stone. . . . The
boy whispers *Mary*. . . . The sudden torment of
his love pierces me. The tear forces itself out of
my eye: it slides hotly, heavily along the coarse
golden curve of my cheek, onto one of the lilies
of the valley, it slides along the bright plastic
stem and onto my left hand, which is slightly
misshapen, too large for a woman's hand, and to

the edge of my hand and off, off into the air, into the candles, into one of the cups. . . . The flame flickers and dies. A short, hissing sound. The boy jumps forward, seems to fall forward. What is he saying? With one finger he touches the rim of the cup, he moves his finger around and around the rim, staring down at the blackened wick, and then he lifts his face to me and stares *and I see again the leaves dying and coming to life again, and again the spiky bushes we must endure, I see the boy living, dying, I see the madness white-rimmed in his eyes, I would shriek with pity and turn from him but I cannot move, the burden of his love has turned me to stone.* . . . He falls to his knees and hides his face. *For me, for me,* he is murmuring. Rocks back and forth on his knees. . . . *For me* . . . he cannot bring his hands away from his face to look at me, he dares not show his face to me, he whispers. . . . *For me? For me* . . . ? He stumbles to his feet, swaying. Backs away with his hands still pressed against his face. Backs along the wall, and now he peers at me again and his eyes grab at mine, he puts out his hand to me in love, in terror, and I yearn to break out of my silence. . . . I yearn to reach up to straighten the tinsel crown on my head, which is a little crooked, and to touch my face, to finger the faint streak down the curve of my cheek from the tear's path, a small rivulet in the grainy wood. . . . I shudder in my long heavy cloak, in the folds of my robe, and I wake to see how they are upon me, crowding upon me, staring, whispering, a jumble of words. . . . *Mary?* a young woman cries. *Mary? Mary? Mary? Mary? Mary?* Her voice is shrill and tremulous. An old woman, her mother, tries to comfort her. But another girl takes up the cry: *Mary?* The young man stands on the edge of the little crowd, near the center aisle of the church, his mother stands beside him humped in black, the priest with him; I hold the Child for their love but they stare past him to my face, to my cheeks, my eyes, they are raging with love for me, only me. . . . Prayers rush upon me, rocking my body, my legs and trunk, my face, bewildering my head, a jumble, centuries of prayers, a tide of prayers, the earth would rock with the passion of their love but I cannot move, my legs would be broad and swift as swords and massive with energy but they are fixed, fixed in place; my robes hang heavily upon me like a winding cloth, I am a small tower inside the granite of the church. . . . Upon my head they are placing a crown of yellow daisies, their fingers are light and adoring and nimble. I can feel the smallest whorls of their fingertips, the secret identities of each of my adorers, ah, how they love me and how piercing, how furious, how terrible is their love! . . . They lift me up onto their shoulders and march up the big aisle to the doors, which are flung back, and the air is bright

with moisture . . . all about me are children
with flowers and the priest and his altar boys
lead us into the glazed light; I see now the outer
wall of the church where vines have grown wildly
since last spring, and the square is turbulent
with people, priests I have never seen before,
strangers with cameras; I see the young man
staring at me, gaping at me, he tries to rush forward but his mother grips his arm, her fingers
close tightly about his wrist; she is a heavy,
stooped woman with reddened, sullen cheeks, a
forehead like wax, so pale, pale with confusion,
fear, I see that she was once a beautiful young
girl and my eyes cannot bear her gaze, her love
and fear. . . . The tear burns like acid in the
boy's heart. *Hail Mary, full of grace.* . . . Murmuring all about me, a tide of murmurs, there
is the odor of manure in the air, moist and acrid
. . . in the cemetery the crosses tilt gray with
centuries of weather and there are bright red
plastic flowers on the graves . . . strangers approach with their cameras; in the procession behind me a boy is playing the trombone, *Don't
love me, don't love* . . . my lips want to open
in a shriek, *Don't love me.* . . . My eyes dart in
fear from face to face and I see everywhere their
love for me, their eyes brimming with love, with
wonder; even at the edge of the cemetery a
woman in the dress of a foreign country stares
and I can see the snarls of her heart, her love

for me in spite of her stiff face, I can see the way my great blue robe and my crown of flowers and the Child in my arms snatches at her heart. *Mary, Mary,* she is pleading silently, and beside her stands a man from the city, studying me and my adorers. . . . Eyeglasses, sharp lines on his cheeks made from grimacing, a long nose, he stares and stares and cannot back away and cannot run forward to kneel; his lips yearn to twist into a sneer and yet they are paralyzed, like mine, his heart is dense with bitter love for me, I would reach out across the mob of heads and shoulders to press my fingers against his lips but I cannot move, I can only hold the Child as always to be adored. . . . Yes, I am named Mary. I am the Mother of God, I am the Virgin with the Child in my arms, in my safekeeping. I am Mary of the Easy Death. I am the Virgin Mary, Mother of God. Everywhere there are patches of sky above me, archways that are pocked from weather; rain-washed granite and iron that is flecked with rust; the fountain by the church wall does not work any longer and is encrusted with the droppings of birds, moss, a green slime that is beautiful against the wall and the dying green of the ivy; flowers of the palest yellow bloom everywhere light as teardrops, light as the touch of thousands of adoring fingers. . . . Now I ride upon a river, a winter of silence. Rainsplotched air, the silence of nights, dark mornings, the murmur of the Mass, the singing, music that twines and rushes around my head, the eyes of my adorers beneath their furrowed brows, so dark and keen with love. . . . What do they see? What do they love? . . . A woman pushes through the small crowd kneeling before me. Like them, she wears black but her face is coarse and reddened. I remember her: she is the young man's mother. Her eyes flicker like the flames in the candles beneath me, maddened, furious, *You are not Mary! You are a thief, a murderer!* she screams. *My son was poisoned by you—they have taken him away—* She pushes her way through the women and runs right to me. With a sweep of her hand she knocks down the burning candles, she screams and grabs at the folds of my robe, she climbs up, her face ruddy with anger, and now someone is trying to pull her down and there are cries and screams that make the day quake. . . . *My son and not yours! Thief! Murderer! Where did they take him, what did you do to him! I want him back, I want him back—* She tugs at the Child in my arms and something breaks, gives way, the Child breaks off— The women are screaming. A man seizes the woman from behind, pulling her down. The Child has broken off, his head and the upper part of His torso, the woman screams and falls backward like a weight and the Child falls with her, heavily to the ground; I have left only half of the Child's body . . . two of my fingers have been torn off . . . the Child's broad flat yellowish face stares up toward me from the ground, no look to it at all, no recognition, it is a doll's wooden face staring up at me. . . . The woman is taken away, I am returned to safety, I stare at the heavy carved doors with my rounded, blank, black-painted eyes, and now someone is repairing me, workmen, the Child is fixed back in the crook of my right arm . . . my fingers are glued back in place . . . the priest supervises my washing, I am scrubbed with small brushes. . . . Now they are gluing a wooden doll into the crook of my arm, now they are painting him and my large, clumsy hand so the crack will not show. . . . But the woman has run away with him, I saw her take him beneath her arm. They are gluing a wooden doll in His place. I must stand like a column with my legs and arms still, a wooden doll with a Moorish cast to his face in my arms, in place of the Son of God. . . . My mother-hood flashed out of me and into her: she weeps and mumbles somewhere, hidden from me, tor-mented to madness by her own motherhood, and I stand here like a column, overlooking the warm glimmering shadows like breaths and the whis-pering beneath me, the whispering that begins again, my glazed black-painted eyes are firm and rounded and blank, darker than the shadows ever get. . . .

The Brain
of Dr. Vicente

The brain of Dr. Vicente has been in its air-cooled compartment now for eighteen months. We communicate with the brain by a chemical and electrical process too complex to explain; one of Dr. Vicente's own inventions, made shortly before his death.

We, the half dozen associates and ex-students of Dr. Vicente's whom he trusted most dearly, think of nothing else but the problem of returning Dr. Vicente to the world. We beg and argue and make threats in order to acquire cadavers—and you can imagine the competition at our Institute—

but when we describe the cadaver-donor to the brain of Dr. Vicente, the brain rejects it.

Of course, the brain cannot see the proposed body and cannot make any judgments based upon the crude sense of sight. Nor can the brain hear, smell, touch, or taste. It communicates to us certain ciphers that are then translated by a computer into our language. For instance, we talked a grieving mother into donating the body of her handsome twenty-year-old son (who was dying from a gunshot wound in the brain—what good fortune!), but when we described this body to the brain of Dr. Vicente it replied in its cipher-language: *Impossible!*

Dr. Vicente was the kindest and most patient of men. He died at the age of sixty-three, of cancer; even at the end of his life, in his misery, he was never difficult and he never spoke to us in so imperious a way. None of us remembers his ever saying *Impossible!*

No member of his family remembers his ever saying *Impossible!*

We find ourselves drifting up to the fifth floor, where the brain of Dr. Vicente lives in its cool, hushed compartment. We speak softly to one another about cadaver prospects in the hospital attached to the Institute—yet why do we speak so softly, when the brain of Dr. Vicente cannot hear us? The brain has no sense organs and therefore no senses. It is a pure brain, it is the essence of the brain Dr. Vicente himself possessed. Nothing distracts it. We approach its compartment and stare through the pane of glass and there is the brain—yes—it cannot know of us staring at it, cannot know of our yearning and our shame.

The Government funded us for a special project in June. We all worked on it eagerly. A cadaver-donor was found who was fifty-nine years old, about Dr. Vicente's height and coloring; the cadaver's face was subjected to a series of complicated operations, each performed by our finest cosmetic surgeon, until it resembled the face of Dr. Vicente—that is, the face he possessed at the time of his death. The surgeon worked with a number of photographs. A perfectionist himself, he wanted to continue the operations until the face exactly resembled that of Dr. Vicente's; only after a bitter argument could he be persuaded to stop.

And then we proceeded to the most difficult part of the project: the installation of Dr. Vicente's brain into this body. The operation took nineteen hours, and its complications and terrors are best forgotten. At last the brain was fixed in the cadaver, and the new Dr. Vicente was invited to contemplate himself in a mirror. Though he had the ability to speak, he did not speak. We decided to leave him alone in the hospital room, with a full-length mirror, and when we returned after fifteen or twenty anxious minutes we found the new Dr. Vicente sitting stiffly with his back to the mirror, his eyes closed. On a piece of Institute stationery was the scribbled word: *Impossible!*

Dejected, demoralized, we returned the brain of Dr. Vicente to its compartment. It exists there now, infinite and pure, without any human distractions. We know that it is thinking constantly, but we do not know of what. Is it remembering the life of old Dr. Vicente?—with fondness, or with contempt? Is it remembering any of us? Is it constructing and resolving monstrous problems, undreamed by other human beings?

Even when we are separated from one another and from the Institute, we think constantly about the brain of Dr. Vicente: it weighs upon us in its silence, its sleeplessness, its three pounds of flesh, its bulges and tubes and delicate silky vessels. We are drawn to its glass door, not by our love for the old Dr. Vicente—who has perhaps died—but by a yearning we do not understand.

Loss

❦

. . . in warm stripes of light, perfectly immobile, the body of a young woman. . . .

V, in her late twenties, came to Rome with her husband, whom she had married after a courtship of hardly more than a year. Her husband was a mining engineer and his work kept him out of the city a great deal; V, knowing no one in Rome, having little to do, began sitting out on the balcony of their flat.

The flat was on the fourth floor of a handsome new building. It consisted of seven rooms, with highly polished parquet floors and ceilings that were ornamental, somewhat old-fashioned in an artificial way, since the building itself had been constructed after the war. One of the bedrooms at the rear of the flat had been converted into an office for V's husband, with a drawing board and a number of bookshelves. The other rooms were conventional in function and appearance. V was especially proud of the sitting room, which opened onto the balcony. In good weather she and her husband had their meals on the balcony when he was home.

At first she missed her husband, thinking that a young wife would miss her husband. Then, as the weeks passed, she began to realize how free she was. Back home, in her parents' house, she had never had much freedom.

Her maid brought breakfast to her out on the balcony. She grew to enjoy the sunlight. She had nothing important to do, and yet she was always busy: writing letters to her mother and her sisters, reading glossy, oversized magazines. Sometimes she allowed herself to be distracted by noises down on the street, so that she sat, motionless, listening, with a small smile, for many minutes at a time.

. . . in the silence of noon, a young woman with the body of a bride, all her movements slow, graceful, contemplative. . . . Her head large and perfectly shaped, like a statue's head, the skull firm beneath the cascading blond hair; the body full, tawny, lazy.

One morning V happened to notice, in the

building adjacent to hers, someone standing at a
glass door facing her balcony. It was a door that
opened onto a balcony also, only a single door,
heavily ornamental. V studied the door and the
figure behind it, wondering if it was a man. Did
he see her? Yes, he must see her. He was standing there motionless, as if hiding.

That balcony was smaller than hers and did
not look as if it were used. Several clay pots had
been set on it, though they contained no plants;
or perhaps their plants had died. The building
itself was quite old, dating back most certainly
to the previous century. It was of a curious green,
muddy color, with a façade V's husband had com-
mented upon once, down in the street, because
it was so mute, orderly, and uninteresting. V had
not really noticed it, even when her husband had
pointed it out; she did not notice most things.
The building was six stories high and its bal-
conies were decorated with dull spikes and spirals,
a masculine style and yet one that looked weary
and heavy. V had the idea that all of the building's tenants were old, solitary, retired people.

She was certain someone was standing there.
Yes. It looked like a man. He was standing there
motionless, evidently watching her.

. . . a woman with a supple, firm body, her
skin gleaming, a woman absolutely at ease be-
cause she wants nothing. . . .

Her lunch was brought to her on the balcony

and afterward she skimmed through a fifteen-page
letter from her married sister in Lisbon. But then,
shyly, she raised her eyes to the window across
the way—at first she could make out nothing,
because the sun had shifted and now the white
light of noon was blinding—then she saw, startled,
that same figure there, dark inside the glow of
light, like a sentry in a box. She stared.

She wanted to jump to her feet and cry out
to him—*Why are you watching me?*

She blushed. She imagined herself as she
must appear to this hidden observer, a surprised,
girlish glow moving up from her throat to her
forehead, out of her control. She wore her hair
pulled back to the top of her head and then tied
with a ribbon, then loose so that it fell thickly
upon her shoulders. She had worn it that way
for fifteen years, though her husband had told
her he did not like it: it was too casual for a
woman of her age. *Blond hair tied tightly and
ascetically at the top of the skull, so that it pulled
the delicate skin around the temples; a few loose
tendrils of hair at the forehead; but then released,
falling down and forward and back, a tumble
of fine glowing blond hair. . . .*

V threw down her sister's letter and got to
her feet angrily. Openly looking at the window
next door, she made a gesture of impatience and
wanted to call out to the man—but she did not
dare call out. Someone else might hear. Also, she

drew back her gesture at the last moment, so that it was not a furious, accusing sweep of her arm, as she had intended it, but a questioning, almost pleading movement, drawn in against her body.

She left the balcony. That afternoon she went out shopping alone. Her mind rang with accusations. She rehearsed the words she would say to her husband: The sunlight was poisoned for her, she could not use her balcony any longer. The next morning she rose early and went to six-o'clock Mass, and was pleased that the day was overcast so she would have no need of the balcony anyway. Afterward she looked through the closed doors at the door in the other building, but no one was there.

Her husband returned the following evening, but V decided not to mention the incident to him. They attended a large dinner party in a hotel, given by the American partners of her husband's employers. V, who had always enjoyed parties, found herself even happier than usual at this party, lightheaded as if intoxicated. But she was certain she was not intoxicated. She understood that she was a beautiful woman; many of the men there gazed upon her with obvious pleasure, as if she were part of the city's exquisite beauty, meant to be appreciated.

And yet it disturbed her from time to time that conversations drifted from her. People were able to enjoy themselves in noisy, heated, complicated conversations V could not follow. V moved from group to group, showing none of her irritation, smiling at everyone, proud that her husband should gaze upon her with such obvious love. He did love her. And yet there was a mystery here, in this group of people. V could not understand it. There was an emptiness, a worthlessness, as when you shake a container and there is nothing inside, a hollowness in her that should be filled.

V found herself standing at the balcony of the hotel suite, staring out at the night. She was distracted, still lightheaded, and when her husband touched her arm she turned to him, startled.

. . . drawn to the sun, to the sun's silence; her robust, full body illuminated by sunlight as if by a loving gaze. . . .

She returned to the balcony. She lay for hours almost without moving, on a lounge chair cushioned with thick pillows; she wore sunglasses. Her entire body was bathed in sunlight, so that she felt strangely weightless, not only suspended in space but in time as well. She was eagerly, anxiously content. Only after a long time did she allow herself to glance over at the other balcony— and then she saw, immediately, that the man had turned. There was no mistake about it. He was standing there, still in shadow, but with his face drawn closer to the glass.

V felt her face go hot.

And yet she did not leave. When her maid served her, she was grateful for the girl's grave efficiency—her mother's servants had never been so efficient, they were all childish and obtrusively humble. V felt that this girl was colorless—a blank, neutral background against which V herself stood out.

Something was going to happen.

When she came out onto the balcony the next morning, she was wearing white. She felt shy, but as the long morning passed, her shyness faded and again she raised her eyes to the balcony next door. It seemed to her that for a remarkable, dangerous instant she was actually looking into the eyes of that stranger. Yet she could not quite make out his face. She felt faint, knowing something must happen. Something was going to happen. Her eyes did not accuse him, but they expressed perfect knowledge of him.

Yes, she knew he was watching. He would know that she knew.

Something was going to happen. *Loose blond hair, a graceful neck and torso, bare arms, a small waist, wide, fleshy thighs. . . .* Her heartbeat quickened. Yet she forced herself to lay her head back against the chair and to close her eyes, feigning sleep.

As the days passed she thought constantly of her hidden observer, and yet she did not really wonder about him. If he had a name, she did not really want to know it. She did not really want to know who he was. His position in life? His age? These questions drifted through her mind idly, with the authority of impersonal questions that might be raised by other women. She herself had no real interest in them. She lay perfectly at ease in the sunlight, feeling the heat release her, so that she did not remember her name and had no concern about the rest of her life.

A new bride, a woman on the threshold of life. White clothing that covered but did not contain her body, her gleaming nakedness; white clothing against warm brown skin. Heat without clarity. When she had to leave the balcony she carried that image of herself in her head. She dreamed of that image. She felt herself as an essence. She felt the soul that was herself like a glow of light, heat that radiated and yet did not explain, a kind of shadow within intense light.

The face perfect in its contours, without thought, fulfilled.

She understood that there is no greater happiness than to be a beautiful woman.

When her husband returned she led him out onto the balcony. There, after an exchange of ordinary information, she began to reproach him suddenly for not loving her, for neglecting her. Her voice grew warm and girlish. Her husband, surprised, began to protest. Of course he loved her—how could she doubt him?

V laughed at him angrily.

Her husband seized her hand. She saw in his face the baffling, violent passion for her that was so pleasing and yet so disturbing. She tried to pull her hand away, insisting he did not love her. He left her alone so much: a man who loved a woman did not leave her alone.

Her husband got to his feet and embraced her roughly. She pushed him away. She felt suddenly as if her soul were in danger of escaping— like a giddy wisp of smoke it was, something that could not be held back.

She rose to push her husband away again, but a curious weakness flowed through her limbs and she sank back into her chair. *Her blond hair would come loose . . . the ribbon would be untied . . . the white dress tugged at, torn. . . .*

She turned her gaze toward the other balcony.

In the morning, alone, she returned to her balcony. She kept her gaze lowered, out of shyness. She saw again and again her body in that embrace, her young husband embracing her, so angrily and so desperately.

She was bare-armed, though the morning was rather cool. The sun was obscured by clouds and the air was slightly bitter. She sat. She had forgotten to bring out something to read. After a long while she returned her heavy-lidded eyes to the other balcony, moving her head slowly and deliberately.

No one was there.

She sat motionless, staring. She waited.

Her eyes seemed to mist over and for a moment she could not see the door clearly—then she saw it again, saw that no one stood there. A hazy light filled the space behind the glass door and it was empty.

She went back into the flat. Later that day she returned as if looking for something—a magazine that had fallen behind a chair—but she did not remain.

The next day she went out again and tormented herself—she would not look at the other balcony, she would not look—but she was unable to stop herself. Her head would turn, her eyes would leap at that door. But no one was there. As soon as she understood this, her heart slowed as if it desired to stop, and her skin felt cool, thin, coated over with the slight bitter film of the city's air, which the sun did not dissolve but only baked onto her body.

She went to Mass again each morning, very

early. She avoided the balcony. She did not even think about it. She sat instead in the comfortable undemanding darkness of the church, trying to illuminate the part of her mind in which she herself existed. She was V, a young woman, a bride. She was loved by her husband. She was a beautiful woman. But for some reason she could not remember herself. She sat and knelt and stood in darkness, absolutely anonymous, a young woman in dark clothing, alone in a large cathedral in a large city.

She closed the balcony off because of the bad air—she complained of the exhaust from the street, which made her eyes sting.

Her husband could not tease her or argue her out of the strange silence she fell into. She could see him well enough and could see the jerking movements of his mouth, but she could not see herself in him. There was no illumination, no picture of herself. She felt her body grow weak, as if emptying out.

She wept because she was going to nothing, becoming nothing. She was frightened. But the fear washed out, emptied itself out, because there was nothing for it to adhere to. She could not explain to her husband, had she the energy to talk to him. On certain mornings, when he was out of town and the sun shone, she did not even get out of bed but lay there beneath the covers.

Loss

The bed covers were heavy and stifling and seemed bunched up around her, as if bunched up about a human body.

Parricide

❦

He is sitting at a long, ungainly table, his thin arms awkwardly folded. As we file into the room he shifts uncomfortably in the straight-backed chair, which is too large for him. Several yards to his left is a window that reaches up narrowly to the ceiling, and it casts onto his face a glow that makes him look stricken, frozen.

Our professor, Dr. Gouveia, dismisses the guard and introduces the three of us—law students in our twenties—to the boy. Dr. Gouveia smiles and the lower part of his face widens. His voice is a softer version of his public voice, used for lectures or in the courtroom; the boy's face imitates his smile at once, but faintly, clumsily.

"You are well this morning, Mário? You slept well last night?" Dr. Gouveia asks, as if prompting the boy.

The boy nods quickly, but heavily. His head seems heavy on his slender neck.

"Yes, you slept well? That's good," Dr. Gouveia says, seating himself across from the boy, who is still nodding faintly, as if hopeful of convincing us all of some falsity. "And did you dream, Mário?"

"No dreams, never," the boy says.

The three of us, three young men, sit at the table self-consciously, and are displeased at its ugly, nicked surface and the fact that one of its legs is obviously shorter than the others. The table will wobble slightly if we lean on it.. The boy glances at us shyly, his lips twitching as if he wanted to smile.

We do not smile at him. My heart begins to pound laboriously, as if I desired something I could not name.

"Yesterday you were explaining to me the man in the field," Dr. Gouveia says, in that same soft and yet buoyant voice, a goodhearted voice that fills the narrow room. "Do you remember?"

The boy shakes his head uncertainly. He does not remember, no.

"The man who approached you in the field. The barefoot man. Do you remember him, Mário?" Dr. Gouveia says coaxingly.

The boy blinks and smiles giddily. He licks his lips.

Fourteen years old.

Thin, with that dark, darkly illuminated skin that stretches across the bones of stark beauty, accenting the bones, drawing attention to the lighter features—the eyes, the eyeballs that seem so white, and the teeth. If he stood he would not be very tall. A child. He is fourteen years old but the edges of his eyes look crinkled, as if worn by severe frowning or squinting or by tears. His hair is thick and dark, closely curled like tiny curls of wire; it would be fine, frizzy, greasy to the touch. The insides of his ears look very white, unnaturally white. But the rest of his skin is of a dark, even ruddy, olive hue, as if the blood just beneath it were coloring it, warming it as we stared.

Dr. Gouveia leans forward, his fingers touching together lightly. He says softly, "Mário, listen to me: the man who approached you in the field—the barefoot man—who came to you with the wood-chopping ax in his hand—did you say his right hand?"

The boy is listening closely. His breath is not rhythmic, but self-conscious, as if he had to remember to breathe. Perhaps it is because of our presence, we three students who cannot help staring. We are neatly dressed, in dark suits and ties. Our hair is neatly combed, unlike the boy's.

We are not so dark as he. We do not smile and blink so childishly as he, but our heartbeats quicken along with his.

The boy lowers his gaze, frowning. He rubs one finger on the table, around and around in a circle. He seems about to speak, but does not speak. Dr. Gouveia waits patiently. The boy moves his finger around and around in a circle, making a dull smudge on the surface of the wood.

He begins to speak in a whisper: "A man—there was a man—ran up to me and said my name out loud—"

"He said your name?" Dr. Gouveia asks.

The boy does not dare glance up. His finger slows, stops. He is perfectly still, like an animal startled in a field, cautious, listening to everything in the air about him, ready to bolt. I can see the movements of his short stubby nose and his lips.

"He said your name, Mário?"

"Mário. Like that. He said my name. He stepped across the furrow and held the ax out to me."

"Yes, and then?"

"And then I was dropping the ax," the boy says, smiling at us. "Then I was inside the house and dropping the ax, I am so clumsy, and it fell on my foot, the edge of the ax on my foot. That was why the blood came to be on my foot."

"Go back, please, to the man in the field.

He said your name and handed you the ax. You reached out to take the ax from him?"

"No. I stared at him, I stood there and did not move. He came up to me. He held the ax out to me and said my name and reached for my hand himself and took my hand in his and pressed the handle of the ax into it and closed my fingers around it," the boy said slowly. After this long speech he smiles at us again, his eyes moving from one face to another.

"Ah, he pressed the handle into your hand, I see," Dr. Gouveia says. "Yes. But you did not remember that before. And he closed your fingers around the handle, yes. And then . . . ?"

"And then . . . the ax fell out of my fingers and hit my foot. . . ."

"You were inside the house when it fell out of your fingers?"

"Yes."

"But you were in the field when the man gave you the ax."

"Yes."

"How did you get in the house with your family?"

The boy's smile fades. His eyes cloud over, the corners of his eyes pucker with thought.

He does not reply.

Dr. Gouveia says again, patiently: "Explain to us, please, how you came to be in the kitchen of your house, with your family, when you had been out in the field working. Did you carry the ax into the house?"

The boy shakes his head wonderingly.

"Yet you found yourself in the house?"

"In the kitchen . . . the ax fell out of my hand and hurt me . . . woke me. . . ."

"It woke you? Out of a sleep?"

"Yes, out of a sleep."

"And what did you see when you woke?"

"The edge of the ax where it hit my foot, I was afraid, I thought how close I was to cutting my foot. . . ."

"And . . . ?"

"And there was all the noise, the little boys. The noise in the kitchen," he says, shrugging his shoulders.

"Your brothers?"

"The little boys, yes."

"Was your mother there?"

He shakes his head.

"No? Or don't you remember?"

"Don't remember."

"Your mother was there, wasn't she? Yes?"

"In the kitchen . . . ?"

"Did your mother cry out to you? What did she say?"

"Don't remember."

The boy's face puckers and then relaxes. He cannot remember.

"Did your father die at once, Mário?"

"I think so."

"Why do you think so?"

"The way the blood came out. Like the pigs, even more blood than the pigs. And he was very still. It was all over. He made no noise but lay there. Some things had been knocked over but now they were still. Some water in a pot spilled . . . went onto the floor . . . but by now it had run through the floorboards and was gone."

"Whose ax was it?"

"My father's. Our ax for chopping wood."

"A man gave it to you and instructed you to go into the house?"

"I don't know."

"He simply gave you the ax?"

"Closed my fingers around it. Hard, so that they wouldn't open again."

"He said nothing to you?"

"My name. Said my name," the boy whispered.

"And then you woke up in the kitchen, with the ax falling out of your hand?"

The boy glances at us, wanting to smile; he looks from one face to the other, seems to linger on my face. I sit very still.

"Do you know the man's name?" Dr. Gouveia says.

The boy sighs as if he has been asked this question many times. "No."

"You had never seen him before, he was a stranger?"

"Yes."

"He was barefoot like yourself?"

"Yes."

"He ran across the field but did not frighten you?"

The boy frowns. "Frighten? Why?"

"With the ax in his hand, a stranger running up to you—he didn't frighten you?"

"I would not be frightened," the boy says slowly.

"Why not?"

"Because I could see, I could see the ax, who it belonged to; I could see it was only our ax."

"And after the man gave you the ax and closed your fingers around it, he went away?"

"I don't know."

"He remained standing there?"

"I don't know."

"He was carrying the ax in his right hand?"

"Yes, the right hand, but with the other hand sometimes touching it when he ran, to steady it. The way you carry an ax." The boy gets to his feet suddenly. We are all startled, especially Dr. Gouveia—but the boy is only demonstrating the carrying of an ax. His right arm sags with its weight; the head of the ax is held high, and the fingers of his left hand touch it as if to balance it.

"Ah, like that?"

"The way you carry an ax," the boy says.

He sits down again. His skin has darkened with embarrassment or pleasure.

"How did he say your name, Mário?"

"Say name . . . ?"

"What did his voice sound like?"

The boy stares at Dr. Gouveia. "A man's voice . . . any voice. . . ."

"Would you recognize it now?"

"Yes. No."

"Why not?"

The boy shakes his head slowly, stupidly. He cannot answer.

"Can you imitate his voice, Mário?"

The boy lowers his head. After several difficult seconds he begins to speak, a murmur, a mutter—"Mário. Mário. Mário."

Because he is looking down at the table I can stare openly at him. My heart is pounding hard; I am tempted to say "Mário" out loud.

Dr. Gouveia changes the topic: "After you dropped the ax, and your father was dead, did you see the strange man again?"

"No."

"What happened then?"

"Then . . . then I was crying like the little boys, like the babies," the boy says painfully, haltingly, "and my mother . . . crying . . . and my uncle that ran in, he put his arms around

46

me. . . . My head went empty again and when I woke up I was in the town."

"And the man did not return?"

"The man . . . ?"

"Yes, the man in the field, he did not come with you? He has not been to see you since then?"

The boy rubbed his finger on the table again, as if Dr. Gouveia's question puzzled him. "Barefoot," he whispered.

"Ah, he was barefoot? And . . . ?"

"And he would not come to town barefoot."

"You told us, Mário, that you did not dream. Do you never dream?"

"Never."

"If you were to dream, what would you dream about?"

He shakes his head, not understanding.

"Would you dream about the man with the ax?"

"There is no face for him. I could not dream him without a face," the boy says.

"You have forgotten his face?"

"No, there was no face to him. Not there."

"Ah, he had no face? No face?"

"No."

The boy looks slyly up at us. From Dr. Gouveia he looks at me, his eyes moving onto me. How I would like to caress him, that dark kinky hair, that dark smooth face! I would caress him into silence.

"The man in the field who approached you, he had no face?"

"Because of the ax. No face."

"What do you mean, because of the ax?"

"How it came down on him, the side of his face . . . the part of it that was sliced off . . . the blood. . . ."

"It split his skull and sliced off part of his face?"

"Yes."

"And there was a great deal of blood?"

"Blood, yes."

"Was the blood on you?"

"No. Dirt."

"What do you mean?"

"Dirt on me. Face . . ."

"There was dirt on your face? Why?"

"From where he rubbed it, to punish me. Also rubbed dirt on me—down here—because I am bad—" the boy whispers, indicating his lap, beneath the edge of the table.

"The man in the field did that to you?"

The boy stares at Dr. Gouveia. He does not seem to understand.

"Why did he want to punish you? Was it that day or some other day? What did he do to you?"

"Because I am bad. . . ."

"Did the man walk with you to the house?"

The boy stares at Dr. Gouveia. "You . . . walk

with me to the house?" he whispers.

"Did the man walk with you to the house?"

"You would walk with me?"

Dr. Gouveia leans forward, peering at the boy. "I am asking you whether the man walked with you to the house where your family was. Did he show you the way?"

The boy shakes his head, baffled. He glances at me out of the corner of his eye—his mouth is slack again and ready to smile.

"You . . . you would walk with me there?" he asks.

Is he looking at me?

"Or you . . . ? Or you . . . ?" the boy asks us, the three of us; but we do not reply.

I can feel him staring at my face. I sit, frozen, waiting for him to release me. I am afraid I will cry out angrily at him—*No, not me, why do you single me out? Murderer! Parricide!*

The moment passes and Dr. Gouveia continues the interview.

The Enchanted Piano

In our house in the city my family had a very large grand piano, many decades old. It was never moved from its place in our second-floor drawing room, before a high, narrow window that faced the street. When I sat at the piano the dull glow from the window would surround me and the hesitant notes of my playing would sound brittle and disturbing, like splinters in the air.

I was forced to begin piano lessons at the age of six; I took them until I was thirteen. But I never played well.

My father had little interest in music and never bothered to check my progress. My mother, who had had lessons before her marriage but who no longer tried to play at all, insisted that I practice every day. Sometimes she sat beside me on the piano bench, sometimes on a couch behind me. Sometimes she was busy in another part of the house but told me that she was listening just the same.

When I was alone with the piano, as I played my lesson slowly, fearful of making errors —if I made the smallest error I forced myself to go back to the beginning—I began to be aware of someone else in the room. I could sense the beginning of something behind me, someone in the back of the drawing room—the beginning of a presence, a shape shaping itself out of the air. When I glanced around, though, I saw nothing. An empty room.

I continued to play bravely. My eyes have always been weak and I had to sit very straight, leaning forward to peer at the book. I whispered the beat aloud. *One* two three. *One* two three. Again and again: and I would feel the shapes pressing gently forward in time with the music. If I did not pause in my playing and did not look around, I would feel the shapes defining themselves more boldly. Did they come out of the floor, or through the rear windows, or down out of the complicated gold and green ornamentation of the ceiling?

They expanded to their full, natural height,

nearly as tall as the room's pillars, and began advancing upon me.

Shapes that were nearly human—like columns, silent, floating—I was aware of them from the corners of my eyes, approaching from behind, behind my head. A terrible fear would rise in me. The shapes advanced under cover of the piano's timid, faltering notes . . . but I had power over them, for as soon as I stopped playing they would draw backward, vanish. When I looked around they were always gone.

I was determined to see them: I would look fully upon them. But my terror always overcame me and I would look back, jump to my feet, sometimes stumbling against the keyboard. At such times I had to press my knuckles against my mouth in order not to shriek.

And then, if Mother did not return and I was alone, absolutely alone, I would sit down again, calm myself, adjust the music book, and begin my piece for the day over again. Again the shapes would appear—I would feel them beginning—and again they would advance silently toward me as I played, protected by the piano's notes. Again they would draw closer. I could sense their tall, urgent, somehow defiant bodies— or the displacement of air that their bodies made— and again I would not dare to continue but would break off suddenly and look over my shoulder—

When Mother was in the room the shapes never appeared.

Once I put a small gilt music box on the piano, its mirrored lid propped up so I could see over my shoulder. When I began playing, the shapes appeared at once; but nothing showed in the mirror. I could almost see them in the corners of my eyes, but I could see nothing in the little mirror.

Light as feathers they advanced upon me, and yet their pressure on the backs of my eyeballs was that of stone: stone monuments, pillars, columns. I remember one piece I had practiced scores of times, and that Mother claimed to love—something called "The Song of May"—and I remember how close the shapes came to me that morning, almost touching me, about to reach out and caress me with their stern, feathery fingers, their arms about to emerge painfully out of the solidity of their bodies—but at the crucial moment my heart lurched with fear and I stopped playing, I threw myself forward against the keyboard, I cried aloud—

Mother hurried into the room. She saw that I was weeping and tried to comfort me. She asked again and again, "Fernandes, why are you crying? Why?" but I could tell her only that I did not want to be loved—never in my life did I want to be loved.

Distance

❈❈❈

When P was twenty-six years old he was honored by an invitation to London, where he worked for his country's embassy. He had a degree in law and had studied international relations, and he came to his first job with enthusiasm and gratitude. Through his associates at the chancery he found an excellent flat with one bedroom, overlooking a square; traffic moved in two continuous streams around this square, and was at first rather disturbing to P, then it became hypnotic and even comforting. His bedroom was at the rear of his flat, on a quiet street.

In Lisbon, P had had to endure a very complicated family life; here, in this large, strange city, he began to realize what a luxury anonymity might be. If his telephone did ring—which was not often—it could not be any member of his family or any friend, inviting him out for an evening or asking favors of him. If his doorbell sounded, it was likely to be someone ringing him in error, looking for former occupants of the flat. Mail found in his mailbox was often for other people; he discovered that several people had recently occupied this flat, so that he himself, rather than being so intensely individualized and even painfully unique, as he had been back home, was in reality one of a series of impersonal tenants. He was grateful for this privacy, which was something new in his life.

Each evening he walked back to his flat from the chancery office; he was intensely interested in the streams of anonymous people around him. Certain streets and intersections were absurdly crowded, yet never with the same people. The city was in a continual flux of change, a kind of convulsion, its fragmented parts oddly harmonious and never combative. In a drizzle of winter like Lisbon's P walked to various parts of the city, stopping at small cafés and restaurants, but never more than once at each, as if he feared being recognized.

He spent his weekends quietly in his flat, grateful for its location and the endless stream of traffic and pedestrians outside: buses, taxis, private cars, trucks, police in raincapes making their rounds. He even noticed, across the way in the park, several men who loitered by a bench. When they remained there most of the day, P realized they were vagrants. At home, such vagrancy would not be allowed; it was something of a shock to see the men there so openly.

There were usually three or four of them. P noticed them from time to time and began to recognize them as individuals, although they were only distinguishable by their clothing. One was an old man in a tan jacket with a kind of fur or false fur collar. Another, also an old man, wore a nondescript coat and a green woollen cap; he thought nothing of lifting his bottle to his lips quite openly, not even hiding the bottle in a paper bag as the others usually did. A third man seemed somewhat younger, perhaps because he was more active, sometimes executing a kind of mocking dance in full view of people who strolled through this end of the park. He wore a dark overcoat. A fourth man sometimes joined them, but only late in the afternoon; he wore a cape-like coat, or perhaps a blanket. He was a shadowy figure and P had no idea how old he might be.

P watched them lift their bottles to their lips without shame. He was surprised and disgusted by them, and he thought them ridiculous.

P withdrew from his window and avoided looking out at the square. He was very pleased

with his flat: it was well-furnished, with a curved
sofa of prickly brown velvet on which he usually
sat in the evenings, reading; a false fireplace made
of plaster, which was not offensive, though it did
not look real; a number of chairs and tables of a
simplicity that contrasted favorably with the ornamentation of his parents' home. His bedroom was
rather large and airy, with long brown velvet
drapes that he rarely closed. He felt very safe
here, and quite at home. He did not even mind
the telephone ringing, since the calls were never
for him and he could explain, quite courteously,
that he was new to the flat and did not know
the former tenants' telephone number or their
location.

One Sunday evening as he sat on the sofa
reading a newspaper, he felt restless and could
not concentrate. So he stood for a while at his
window, looking down at the traffic and the men
in the park just across the street. He wondered
at the contrast between these homeless men and
the people who strolled past them, obviously
well-to-do tourists from nearby hotels. There was
a peculiar difference between them: not only the
relative immobility of the vagrants and the
mobility of the strollers, but the difference in
shapes, which P found difficult to comprehend.
The vagrants were somehow inert and shapeless;
the tourists well-defined, always keeping to the
path and never pausing. The women took firm

hold of their companions' arms and, after the first surprised glance, did not look toward the vagrants.

P watched as two policemen walked past, but they did not seem to notice the vagrants. He was disappointed and rather angry with them, and wondered if it was the custom in this country to allow such open drunkenness. This neighborhood was an excellent one; P had been congratulated on his good fortune, especially since the park was so close. But now he thought bitterly that the park was spoiled for him by these men. He really did not want to go over there, even in sunny weather.

Yet it was unthinkable that these men should prevent him from enjoying the park: and so he deliberately went over, to assert himself. Because the boulevard was so busy, it was necessary for him to take a pedestrian underpass. This tunnel was well-lit, yet quite dirty and unpleasant. Crowds of pedestrians swarmed through it in both directions; P found that he had to move along quickly or he would be jostled. A young man with very long, untidy hair played the guitar for passers-by, and a girl held out a sack for donations, shaking the sack in time with the music so that the coins jingled. P stared at them, offended at such public begging. Very few pedestrians paused even to glance at them, but hurried by as if they had seen or heard nothing. What was puzzling was the young man's obvious enthusiasm: he seemed to play the guitar quite well, and his singing voice was fresh and rather attractive. The girl smiled dreamily at everyone who passed, as if she did not really expect much attention.

P emerged into the daylight on the other side of the boulevard, feeling a little disoriented and irritable. He allowed the swarm of pedestrians to pass by him so that he could see the vagrants on their bench. As always, they were drinking openly; one sat not on the bench but on the grass, his legs parted, and he seemed to be singing. P stared in disgust. Someone bumped into him, muttered an apology, and hurried on. P stood off to one side, so that he would not be disturbed in his angry contemplation of these men. He half feared they would notice him, yet in a way he did desire their attention, for then they might sense how despicable they were in his eyes, and shame might force them away from this corner of the park. He would not mind, he thought, if they spent their time elsewhere: their lives were their own to destroy, after all. But it was unthinkable that they should behave in this disgusting fashion, so that his view from this window was ruined.

The man he had thought to be fairly young was, in reality, middle-aged. He sat on the bench, leaning forward. He was carrying on a long, laconic, drunken argument with the man who sat on the ground. A third man, perhaps in his sixties, in the tan jacket with shaggy trim, did not appear to be listening to the other two; he lifted the paper bag that hid his bottle, and seemed to be winking at P over the rim.

P's face burned with embarrassment. He was really quite angry. He would never have rented the flat, excellent as it was, had he known these men would be stationed in the square. In fact, he would have liked to call attention to them by addressing strangers who passed by, especially the well-to-do American tourists, who might then complain to the authorities; very ironically, mockingly, he would say: "And what do you think of these examples of humanity? Very attractive, aren't they?" But of course he did not dare speak to anyone.

Back in his flat, standing at the window, he watched as the sun went down and the men's figures became indistinct. Their blending with the shadows seemed to him sinister, as if the dark were simply an extension of their own shapeless anonymity.

That was what offended him most: their absolute namelessness and the unlikelihood of their ever having possessed names. There was an odd freedom in their inert bodies, a formlessness in their faces that other people could never imitate. Therefore they were invulnerable, in a still, dead, nasty way.

But P's anger toward them left him listless and oddly discouraged. He stood at the window and sipped brandy and thought with relief of Monday, when he would be at work.

Yet the next morning he felt unaccountably tired. It was an effort for him to bathe and dress, and the walk to the chancery was cold and unpleasant. Once there, he felt feverish; he was told to take a taxi home and go to bed. He argued feebly that he did not want to return to his flat, that he preferred to work. But in the end he surrendered and allowed someone to hail a taxi for him.

He went immediately to bed, avoiding the living room and the window. But at four-thirty in the afternoon he woke, suddenly restless, and wandered out without quite thinking of what he was doing. He found himself staring across at the men, all four of them, and his heart pounded angrily. He was not hungry, though he had not eaten all day. He poured himself a small drink, brandy of the kind he had had sometimes at home, and stood at the window while the long afternoon darkened. It began to rain. Good, he thought. He pressed his face against the glass, wondering if the rain would drive the men away; perhaps underground, into the pedestrian underpass. There, people would surely take notice of them and they might be arrested. Yet the men did not seem to mind the rain at all. They were quite alone in the park now, and brazen in their drinking. One of them did a foolish mocking dance in front of the others. P wondered at the contrast between them and decent human beings— the distance between himself and them, though only a boulevard separated them.

He did not bother to go out to a restaurant, but remained in his flat, drinking slowly. He was really not hungry. He went to bed early, feeling dizzy and disoriented, but a long night's sleep did not refresh him and he decided, shakily, not to go to work that day. Instead he telephoned the chancery and, having made his excuse, decided that he would not let his feverishness or the presence of the men in the park make him unhappy; on the contrary, he would establish his own mood. He would drag the sofa over to the window and lie there, in order to keep a check on those men. He felt they would go away sometime soon and this would gladden him immensely; it was important that he know the exact minute of their departure.

He lay on the sofa with a blanket over him, sipping brandy. When the brandy ran out he opened a bottle of dinner wine. It was not until two o'clock in the afternoon that he supposed he should rouse himself, to go down to the foyer and see if he had any mail. He did not really want to go down, but he felt he should; he was expecting a letter from home.

Moving slowly, he went to get his mail, and was annoyed to see that the single letter for him—there were two others in his mailbox, addressed to strangers bearing his address—had been rumpled. It had obviously been allowed to get wet. His name and address, written in his mother's clear, sloping hand, and in the dark blue ink she always used, was a little smudged.

P brought the letter upstairs and for some reason went into his bathroom to open it. The words danced and made him dizzy; he tried to read them, but could not. He supposed that in a few minutes his eyesight would clear and he could read the letter. But in the meantime he did something odd and experimental: he let a few drops of water fall from the faucet onto the letter. The handwritten note began to smear. Droplets of blue ran into the sink, even over his fingers; it was fascinating to watch.

In the end the letter was unreadable, the ink had run everywhere, and the words had become shapeless. Though he brought the letter to the window and tried now quite earnestly to read it, he could not. In exasperation he crumpled the letter and threw it into a wastebasket.

The next morning he rose, got dressed, and crossed immediately over to the park. Again he passed the young man with the guitar, who sang as freshly and as exuberantly as before, though no one appeared to be listening to him. The girl, dressed this morning in a long pink gown, shook her meager sack of coins and gazed vacantly at the faces of the passers-by, taking no more notice of P than of anyone else, though he stared at her quite openly. Could they be insane, these young people, to station themselves in this dirty, crowded tunnel?

P climbed the steps to the sidewalk and approached the corner of the square where the men sat. There were only three of them this morning. P approached them more slowly now, his anger becoming shy, a little fearful. He really did not have anything in mind. Suddenly aimless, he sat on a nearby bench and watched them. The oldest man, in the tan jacket, glanced at P from time to time, but evidently did not find him a threat. Perhaps because he can see I am not English, P thought suddenly, with a flash of shame; perhaps he does not think I matter.

Though he was so much closer to them, in fact only a dozen yards or so away from them, he could not make out their faces well. Vague, blurred, somehow formless masses of flesh: pale, mottled with red flushes, sickly, slack, ugly, yet not clearly defined faces with individual, detailed features. Even the man in the dark overcoat, who was singing noisily to himself and whose eyes were pouched and mocking, seemed to possess no special face; P doubted that he would have recognized him anywhere else, apart from this corner of the park.

P sat for nearly an hour, watching them. They ignored him. After a while he stood, stiffly, feeling himself rebuffed. He went back to his flat, angry and confused, wondering if they scorned him because he was not English. In his bathroom mirror he saw a rather pale, distraught young man who had forgotten to shave for two days. Obviously a foreigner!

He drifted back to the window, and some change in the wave of traffic—a near-accident between a bus and a small sports car, similar to a red car P himself owned back home—jolted him into an awareness of what he was doing. He had stayed home again from work; he was unshaven, unclean, strangely dizzy; it was obvious that he was not well. He felt a flash of panic.

He must control this absurd fascination: must control the domination of the vagrants over his life.

For two days, therefore, he did not look out the window. He went back to work, worked well, and when he returned he avoided the window; he stayed in his bedroom. He did not even answer the telephone when it rang. But on the third day, terribly restless, he told himself that he must check to see if the men had drifted away yet. As soon as they disappeared he would be well again; a terrible burden would have been lifted from him.

But they were still there, as usual. In fact, the fourth, shadowy figure had joined them, seated on the ground. P stared and wondered if that other person might not be a woman. . . . He shuddered with disgust: a woman!

He realized that he must put himself in control of this situation. He might do any number of things: approach the men directly and give them money, like any charitable but slightly misguided well-wisher, which would result in their leaving the park and taking up residence in some cheap hotel, perhaps. At any rate they would leave the park, he felt certain. Yes, perhaps he would give them money. He could give them fifty pounds—a hundred pounds! His gift would astonish them.

But then other vagrants might take their places. Three other men, and a shadowy fourth who would come to join them in the late afternoon, wearing a cape, perhaps a woman. . . . What then? What if new vagrants appeared? What if he discovered, after painful scrutiny, that they were really the same men, come deliberately back to the square in order to extort more money from him and torment him?

He felt he would go mad.

But there was something else he could do: he could offer money to someone and request that these vagrants be killed. He could pay well for their deaths.

Yet in this strange city he knew no one, he knew no one to contact, he had not the first idea of how to go about so desperate a venture. . . .

It would be easier, P thought ironically, to kill himself.

In the end he got dressed again and went down through the underpass, half noticing the boy with the guitar and the girl with the sack of coins, having no time for them. He went to sit near the men, carrying a bottle of dinner wine in a paper bag, and pretended not to be concerned with them. He could overhear their muttering, a kind of perpetual, formless flow of words, not exactly an argument, in fact almost affectionate, though he could not make out what they were saying. Were they talking about him? Were they wondering who he was?

He wondered how long it would take to cross the distance between them, between their bench and his. Only a few yards, yet an all but overwhelming distance; he would have to be humble and patient and give no sign of his agitation.

In a Public Place

❦

Here is the lobby of the famous hotel you visit
often for your amusement and have memorized:
large, sturdy sofas and chairs of black leather
and a dull checked fabric, beginning to show
wear, arranged in uniform rows at the start of
each day, leading out from two walls, with an
aisle of perhaps twelve feet in the center, sepa-
rating them. Dark, highly polished mahogany.
Plants the height of men, which appear to be
artificial but are, in fact, living in ornate gold-
trimmed vases. Near the arched doorway there
is usually activity, but back farther in the lobby
everything is quiet. People walk lazily up and
down the carpeted isle, glancing at those who

are seated, most of them older gentlemen, groggy
with disuse. Music is being piped in, the same
furry, glazed texture as the carpet; the music
seems to be coming from a great distance and
no one is listening to it. A few men are speaking
softly to one another, but most are silent and
solitary. Velvet drapes have been drawn over
the windows that face the ocean, in order to
eliminate the sunset.

Because it is so public a place several men
are sleeping openly, like infants, lying back in
the enormous leather-armed chairs that hold them
firmly. There is an undeniable strength in the
heavy clawed feet of the chairs. Nothing can
happen here, the sleeping men believe, because
in their sleep they are anonymous, like all
travelers, having left their homes and not yet
having arrived at their destinations, where they
will be recognized. There are twelve rows of
chairs with eight chairs in each row; as usual,
perhaps thirty or thirty-five of these chairs are
occupied, though only about six men are sleeping
this evening. On the walls are immense dark
paintings of forest and sea scenes, filled with indistinct crowds of people or animals: no one
looks at these paintings, perhaps because they
appear so dark, so impenetrable.

You walk slowly along the aisle, your eye
moving experimentally over the faces of the sleeping men. You choose a man quite arbitrarily,

because the mechanical music reaches a con-
clusion and comes to a ten-second pause just
as you pass his chair.

This gentleman believes himself invulnerable, lying heavily back in a chair in the lobby
of a famous hotel, his feet out solidly before him,
his face sagging contentedly in sleep. On his lap
is an opened book. His hands are folded over it;
his body in that suit of fine though slightly rumpled light wool is heavy, the stomach and thighs
thickened as if sleep exaggerated them. Sixty-
five years old, perhaps. Neatly brushed gray hair,
surprisingly thick. A small mouth, pursed shut.
He does not remind you of anyone you have
ever known.

You circle him slowly. Only three seats away
is another gentleman in his sixties, reading a
foreign-language newspaper. He doesn't glance
at you. Two rows behind him is an elderly couple,
the man dozing off, the woman expressionless,
though she is facing you. Now the music begins
again, dimly, like an extension of the sleepers'
vague, unimportant dreams.

You consider your victim from his left side—
his profile is that of a stubborn man, though the
chin is bunched flabbily against the stiff collar
of his shirt. You cross to his other side and consider him again—the peevish contentedness of
a sixty-five-year-old infant. In the subdued light
of the lounge all the finer wrinkles of his face

are obscured. His skin therefore appears tender. His breath is hoarse and occasionally breaks to a soft snore, then drops again, absorbed into the recorded music. You could imagine something about this man's life, based on his clothes and his heavy, stubborn features, but you do not have time.

You wait for two men to pass by, headed for the arched doorway and the outer lobby. They do not notice you and you make no effort to overhear their whispered conversation, which cannot concern you.

Now you approach your victim and seat yourself beside him, so lightly that your chair does not even squeak. You note that he is sleeping quite deeply; he has no awareness of you or anyone else. Out of your inside coat pocket you draw a length of very fine wire, perhaps two feet long. In a single swift movement you loop the wire around the sleeping man's neck, and, not hesitating even for an instant, you tighten the wire into a noose. You pull hard at the ends of the wire, crossing your hands; the man's eyes pop open and his torso heaves upward. But you hold him down firmly. After some seconds of tense, muscular struggle, during which the book falls onto your feet, the wire seems to have disappeared into his flesh and he sags back into his chair, still.

Nearby a stroller pauses to light his cigar; behind you the old woman seems to be watching you, though perhaps not—her eyes may be closed. In an armchair pushed back against a wall an old gentleman lets his newspaper drop, sighs, clasps his hands beneath his protruding stomach, and surrenders to sleep.

You undo the noose with some difficulty, and put it back into your pocket. You pick up the book and lay it back, opened at any page, on the old gentleman's knee.

For a while you sit in the lobby beside your victim, contented, with that strange, pleasing inertia of public places in which no one speaks above a whisper. The utter safety of such a place is a kind of oblivion: in such reservoirs of civilization you understand that you are immortal.

The Seduction

❧❧

You look over your shoulder to see who is following you.

But there is no one. You continue to walk more quickly. At a corner you pause, as if without calculation, and again glance behind you—still you see no one, nothing.

Yet *he* is in the air around you, almost visible. You must resist the impulse to swipe at the air around your head, as if driving away gnats, which you cannot quite see. You are terrified of someone noticing you, remarking upon your agitation. It is a frightening thing to be on the street like this without a companion; a man alone, however conventionally and handsomely he is dressed, is vulnerable to any stranger's eyes.

As you cross a busy street, obeying the traffic policeman's baton, *he* glides behind you, his feet barely skimming the cobblestone street. He is light, airy. You will not be able to shake him in all this traffic. Does he sing in the air around your head, a high, shrill, barely audible song? You walk faster, yearning to escape.

You fear that he will ease into your head, a perfect fit.

He will argue with you about a certain street, a certain square where the short, fine grass grows on a slope, where an aged fountain sends its spurts of water brightly into the air. Facing the square is a building with a high granite wall surrounding it and a gate adorned with small gold crosses. There are exactly six stone benches in this square. You cannot mistake it. You remember it clearly.

But you turn away, you flee across the city and into the hills of the city. That square is miles behind you. When you arrive at your destination you think of the narrow, sloping streets that surround you and divide you from him, the maze of streets that are symbolic of the complications of your life. Yet it is an adult's life and it must be kept under your control.

You are pleased to think of these complications. The square and the bench he is sitting at and his face, which you keep carefully blank in your mind's eye, refusing to give it life, his being, his presence, have nothing complicated about them: they are simple. All human life is simple, in itself. Simplicity is vulgar and you will resist it, because you are an adult.

The warm mass of a woman's body: this is your destination.

You have arrived at your destination, and it is accorded you a certain greeting. The woman is genuinely surprised. She says, "You look exhausted—are you ill?"

No, but you are staggering with the complications of your life.

"You must sleep. You must sleep," the woman says softly, commandingly. You accept the pronoun "you"; it is a pleasure to accept it; it should be a pleasure, yet you still feel the swarm of that other presence, and as if to escape it you press yourself into her arms. She embraces you and will lie awake while you sleep, to protect you. There is tenderness between you, but it is only courtesy.

You hear your own voice: "I can't sleep. I need to keep awake."

"No, you must sleep," she says.

You must sleep, like this, in a woman's arms. It does not matter which woman. These are your instructions and it is obvious that they are perfect instructions. If you disobey them you will be thrown back upon yourself, running backward through the day, the traffic, back to a square on the far side of town, with your hair fallen onto your forehead and your mouth dry, yearning. Someone will rise from a bench in that square and reach out to seize your parched tongue, which is like a dog's loose exposed tongue, and he will give you a rough shake by way of a greeting.

You want to ask the woman, *Why must I sleep?—why must I sleep in a woman's arms?*

She is too simple, too ignorant, to exclaim the truth, which you already know: *There is no other sleep possible.*

You try to obey. But obedience is difficult and your heart pounds; it pounds as if you were exerting it, hurrying back across the city, while in fact you are lying quite rigid. You press your tongue hard against the dry roof of your mouth so that you will not cry out unexpectedly against this imprisonment. Far better this room with its ordinary wallpaper, an ordinary clean house and street that you need not take any special notice of—far better these human, womanly confinements than the openness of the street, the city, the square, the rustling of air about your face that is a continual torment to you.

Your eyes are closed. You force a dream upon yourself, as you did as a child, but the dream is not of this woman: instead it is of swinging arms and hands, somehow your own arms and hands, and yet a stranger's, *his*, so that you are forced in the dream to glance down at your own body and see that it belongs to him. The hands with their long perfect fingers, the shoes of dark, highly polished leather, the black shoe-laces with their black tips that seem to be made of plastic: none of these belong to you. They are his. They await you patiently somewhere in the city.

It is a mistake, you want to shout down the length of that body, which is your body but also his, his body but also yours. It is a mistake. You must sleep here, in this woman's arms, and nowhere else. Only here can you realize your distinctness: you cannot ever become her, or she you, in even the most damaging of nightmares. You will lie here, you will not break away. You will not run to that square. You will lie very still, and you will finally sleep. When sleep comes it will be a perfect sleep, because it will be achieved in a woman's arms, where no emotions are possible.

Maimed

✠

Like everyone else, you live in a place where people love you and where it is their duty to love you. Though administered with a sigh, their love is nevertheless real. You will never lose it.

Once you leave the house in which you live, however, you leave all love behind. You risk everything. Those who love you avoid your eye, brushing at your clothes, whispering half-affectionate, half-scolding commandments: Stand proudly, with your shoulders back. Brush your hair from your forehead. Wipe your nose. Exchange that handkerchief for a clean one. What are you thinking of, to walk out like that? Why do you want to go out at all?

Maimed

At the last moment their eyes lift to your face. You see the small flinching frown that means they are hoping for a change in you—what a futile hope! They are hoping that somehow, overnight, you have become a normal person, and that they do not need to fear for you.

They watch you through the front windows as you walk along the sidewalk out into the city.

You carry a certain disfigurement with you everywhere you go. It is impossible to hide it. You have no direct knowledge of this disfigurement; your knowledge is derived only from the faces of passers-by. On an ordinary day—for instance, a Monday morning, when the air happens to be fresh with rain—you leave for your walk, remembering to walk proudly, because after all you have been dressed in decent clothes and have nothing to be ashamed of, and for the first several blocks you walk quickly enough, like anyone else out for a morning walk; then, when the faces begin to crowd your vision and certain small muffled exclamations come to your attention, your stride begins to falter and you remember that question put to you so solemnly in your home: *Why do you want to go out at all?*

Sometimes you must excuse yourself, making your way nervously through a small curious group that has gathered on the sidewalk. Difficult to say whether they have gathered because of you, or because it is in their nature to stand about like this, waiting for anything out of the ordinary to entertain them. You don't ask them, of course, shying away from their stares and their occasional awed grins, especially shying away from the children, who sometimes point boldly and cry out, *Look!*

These children would be your salvation if you dared ask them exactly why they are pointing at you. But you never ask.

You obey a perfectly rigorous and sensible strategy: you walk a number of blocks in one direction, then in another, then in another, until you have completed a kind of rectangle around the house in which you live, and then you return to the house. You are safe there. You have only this time to ascertain, by your readings of the faces on the street, exactly what the nature of your disfigurement may be. Certain clues are offered from time to time—a sudden uncontrollable tremor in a woman's cheek, which might perhaps be in sympathy with a similar abnormality in yourself; the involuntary gesture of a man who touches his lips, as if, in seeing something deformed about your lips, he is checking his own. But you cannot be certain. There is bound to be an unavoidable margin for error in this kind of analysis and, also, over the years so many clues have been suggested to you that you are at a loss to evaluate them, discarding the worthless and cherishing the significant.

Maimed

On certain mornings you return home out of breath and exhilarated, having taken in a number of vivid, convincing clues; on other mornings you return home dismayed by the rude and unhelpful gawking of people on the street, who, it seems, have never seen anyone quite like you and do not consider you a human being like themselves.

As soon as you enter your home you are safe. Everyone is loved in your family, more or less equally, and it is not likely that here you will ever be stared at cruelly. No one will point at you. No one will grin in surprise. Here you will never discover the precise nature of your disfigurement; not even the most innocent gaze will suggest it. You are safe. Even the mirrors will not tell you your secret.

You are safe in your home and yet it is the street you yearn for and dream about: the night is bearable only because of the morning, when you will venture out into the street.

Two Young Men

❦

1940

Perhaps out of loneliness, F became very religious at the age of twenty-three. He went to Mass nearly every day, at different churches in the city. He had the idea that his loneliness would be obscured by the fact of his going to a different church as often as possible; that way, it was never a surprise that he knew no one.

He found it impossible to sleep more than three or four hours each night. Lying awake, he thought about the classes he attended, imagining himself helpless and small as a child, dwarfed by the American students. Though he knew English well, the strain of using this language constantly exhausted him. He could not hide from it. Here, English was a medium which everyone used instinctively and in which everyone made his way without effort. F's knowledge was only intellectual and belonged to the most superficial part of his brain. He was not buoyed along by the invisible motions that kept others afloat. Therefore he yearned to be alone so that he could be safe; but, once alone, he felt keenly his separateness and was ashamed. To comfort himself, he began saying certain prayers and performing certain rituals which he had invented as a child and had largely forgotten since then.

His room was a small, decent room on the top floor—the fourth floor—of a handsome brownstone house. He did not know the other residents, though they were obviously students or instructors at the University. Frequently F listened to the various indistinct sounds that went on all night, conversations and the noise of radios and phonographs, all made by strangers, and he wondered why he had come so far for his studies when he could as easily have remained in Europe. When he had an especially unpleasant night, he rose before six and went to six-o'clock Mass; there was no question of his remaining in bed beyond eight o'clock, because workmen who were remodeling a building next door began work at that time. The hammering made him frantic.

The Poisoned Kiss

One morning in December, when it was still dark and an abrasive, slanted rain was falling, F dressed and hurried out to a large, cavernous church some blocks away, and attended Mass with no more than ten or twelve other people, most of them older women. They were scattered throughout the gloomy church, as if their essential loneliness were a delicate and private matter which they did not want to violate. F was the only young man. He felt his usual relief as he knelt at prayer, his hands pressed against his tired eyes and pulling down firmly upon the flesh of his cheeks. He could hold his entire face in his hands at such moments; he might have been examining himself dispassionately.

He was a lean, olive-complexioned young man with slightly hollow cheeks and a habit of sliding his fingers up under his glasses in order to press them against his eyes.

At the communion rail, F was given the Eucharist by an old, balding priest with an apologetic stoop to his shoulders. The altar boy, who was about ten years old, his eyes glittering with the early hour and his hair still damp from combing, stared too intently at F, as if guessing at his foreignness.

After Mass, F left the church reluctantly. He could see through the tall, heavy doors that were closing and opening, how unpleasant the day had become. He was really reluctant to leave the church. He happened to glance at a man walking on his right, and they exchanged a brief, polite smile, a kind of silent confirmation of the poignancy of the moment—that moment when one must leave a church for the drabness of an ordinary morning.

Outside, the man stopped F. "Are you a stranger here?" he asked.

F smiled shyly, uncertainly. He nodded.

"I thought so! I've never seen you here before, at least not at this Mass. I have a habit of this Mass myself," the man said. He fell into step beside F. "Which parish do you belong to? Or are you new to the city?"

"Since September," F said.

"Where are you from?"

"Lisbon."

"Ah, Lisbon! Lisbon," the man exclaimed. His smile flashed and faded. "I've never visited Lisbon, but . . . but I understand it's one of the most beautiful cities in Europe . . . And you're a student here? And you're alone? You don't know anyone here?"

F hesitated. He did not know what to say.

F looked quickly at the man, and then away —he was startled by the man's new, broad smile, which was out of all proportion to smiles F had experienced here from strangers. This man was middle-aged, with a plump, bulbous nose and rather arched eyebrows, though his eyes were small, serious, and intelligent; he was exceptionally well-dressed, in a dark overcoat.

"Where do you live? Is it far from here? A long hike?" the man asked.

F began to reply, stammered, and fell silent.

"Is English difficult for you?" the man asked gently.

"No. Yes. Somewhat difficult," F said.

They walked together in silence for nearly a block. Evidently the man was headed in the same direction as F. F's heart had begun to pound in alarm and he did not want to glance sideways at his companion, who might still be smiling that broad, insistent smile; in fact, F believed he could hear the wet crinkling noise made by the man's mouth as it stretched, his lips stretching and parting over his front teeth.

"I'm new to Cambridge myself," the man said. "I'm not connected with Harvard officially yet, but there is a distinct possibility that I will be offered an appointment next semester. . . . My immediate problem is: boxes of books! There must be a hundred cartons of my books, still unpacked, in the house I've rented." The man gestured helplessly. "Can you imagine books in piles on the floor, and more books in boxes and cartons, blocking my hallway and halfway up the stairs . . . ? It would be quite worthwhile for anyone . . . any young man . . . I mean a husky young man like yourself, if . . . if he

might oblige me by helping me unpack them.
. . . I would be willing to pay you generously.
We might both put on overalls and sweaters and
unpack the books, just jump right into the task
and get it finished at last, though we could certainly stop for lunch. . . . Are you agreeable?
Would this be an interesting way of spending
the day?"

F looked directly at the man and saw, in
his small, shrinking eyes, his own loneliness pro-
jected there.

"I have a class at eight o'clock," F said.

He must not have spoken clearly, for the
man did not seem to understand.

"You have difficulty with English?" he said
brightly, putting his hand on F's arm. "Don't
you understand everything that is said to you?
Don't you understand?"

F jerked away from this touch. He hurried
from the man, and in spite of himself he began
to run, like a child. One block away he dared
look back over his shoulder and there the man
stood as if paralyzed—in his black overcoat, in
the drizzle, staring after F.

F went back to his room and stood at the
window, staring out into the street, until the
workmen began hammering next door. He never
returned to that church again. He understood
the man might be waiting for him.

The Poisoned Kiss

1971

F, leafing through museum catalogues, through aged books and encyclopedias, through piles of old photographs, was dry-mouthed with wonderment. What was he seeking? What had he lost, that he must seek it so desperately?

He visited his sisters and brothers, under the pretext of wanting to see his young nieces and nephews. Here, in these large, pleasant homes, he was Uncle F, who so rarely came to visit. He spent afternoons wandering through the corridors of these big old homes, examining the portraits on the walls. Coarse, fading, too-fleshly human beings, ancestors of his, but without meaning. . . .

Had they been able to shrug themselves into life, awakened by his intensity, they would surely not speak any language he could understand.

One of his sisters lived in the townhouse their parents had lived in and F felt most at home here. At first he was dismayed that some renovation work was going on in one wing of the house; the hammering and sawing noises made him nervous. But when he glanced through the plans for the "modernization" of this part of the house, and after his sister explained enthusiastically what would be done, he felt a kind of excitement. He began to visit the workmen, to watch them at work. He knew nothing about carpentry and was fascinated by the carpenters' efficiency. He was drawn to the activity there, the busyness of the man in charge—who was exaggeratedly deferential to F—and the silent, brisk work of the several young carpenters.

One of them, who was hardly more than a boy in his early twenties, answered F's questions quietly and shyly, always lowering his gaze as if in the presence of someone very important. F was honored by the young man's courtesy. He wore workman's clothes, but they did not seem so soiled and ill-fitting as those of the other carpenters.

"Have you done this kind of work for very long?" F asked.

"Ten years. More. I worked with my father in the beginning," the young man said.

"Ten years! And do you enjoy your work?"

"Yes. Very much," the young man said gravely, and F could see that this was a sacred topic to him.

F looked forward to the arrival of the workmen in the early morning. He had a light breakfast, no more than coffee and rolls, and went downstairs to watch the work. He always had a compliment or a suggestion to make; he carried news back to his sister, who avoided that part of the house because of the noise and the odor of fresh wood, to which she believed she was allergic. F had grown to like the smell very much.

He liked also the fresh, wet, oysterlike smell of plaster.

He strolled about, careful to keep out of the workmen's way, and often lingered by the young man in order to ask him about his family. The young man had several children, one of whom had a weak chest; F always inquired about the child's health.

One afternoon, shortly before the workmen were to leave for the day, F took the young man aside and said, in a low voice so that the others could not hear and be jealous, that he would like someday soon to visit the young man's home. Would this be possible? F complimented the young man on the work he had done here and explained that he would like to show his appreciation, privately, quite apart from what his brother-in-law would pay for the work. The young man was embarrassed and seemed unable to say anything. F went on quickly to say that he would be honored to meet the young man's wife and children, whom he almost felt he knew, and if he could help out in any way . . . ?

"I hope I'm not embarrassing you," F said. "That is the last thing I intend. . . ." He wondered at his tone, his frankness. It was so difficult to avoid condescension and yet to avoid a false show of equality that would be even more offensive. . . .

"I'm not embarrassing you?" F asked.

"No," the young man said shyly.

"Perhaps I could visit with you now? Simply walk with you, and make no fuss about a special visit?" F asked. "I would like that very much— I don't want to upset your wife with the trouble of a visit. I'd be honored just to see your family as they are. . . ."

"Yes," the young man said.

F went up to his room to get a coat, but when he returned the young man was not downstairs. F asked one of the other carpenters where he had gone. Evidently the young man had gone outside; he must be waiting outside. F hurried out into the street, looked up and down, and saw the young man, in his workclothes, walking quickly away. What was wrong? F wanted to break into a run and follow him. But instead, his heartbeat suddenly suffocating, he called out the young man's name in a voice that made several passers-by turn to stare at him. The young man, half a block away, looked back over his shoulders and, though he seemed to see F clearly enough, he did not stop.

F called out his name again.

But the young man had now turned the corner.

What was wrong? F stood out on the sidewalk for several minutes, perspiring nervously, staring after the young man. He kept seeing the young man's outline there, above the sidewalk, just at that moment when he was about to turn the corner and disappear: a frail, shimmering outline, yet absolutely stable. F feared it would always remain there, at the corner of this street he knew so well, that he had known for nearly fifty years.

The Secret Mirror

You are alone in your rented room. You are alone before your full-length mirror, which is on a large, cumbersome mahogany stand so that it can be tipped one way or another, according to your desire. You adjust it with a touch of your fingers—just so—exactly so. But when you let go, the mirror eases back into its old position as if taunting you.

No matter. First, the copper-colored curls, a gentle explosion of light. You fit the cap snugly onto your head, stretching the elastic band around the perimeter of your scalp. It fits perfectly. The coppery curls will move in the wind, they will bounce and tickle your face. You stare at the curls in the mirror and a cry escapes you—an exclamation of surprise and pleasure.

The curls were put on too quickly, too eagerly, and now they will get in the way of your other things. But you hesitate to take them off when they fit so perfectly. The elastic band might break, or lose its resiliency.

Now the undergarments, the secret garments. You dress yourself slowly. All your things are white and with white you must move slowly. You raise your arms as if in a ceremonial gesture, in order to slide the white silk slip down over your head. It glides down upon you gently. A faint odor of perfume about it, though you have brought no perfume here. The white of the slip is very white and seems to glow in the mirror, a brightness disturbing to the eye.

A single strand of copper-colored hair floats down, down to the floor. You watch it fall, not breathing.

The stockings are a pale brown and they will hide the terrible pallor of your legs. The ugliness of your legs! It is difficult to resist the impulse to hurry now, drawing the stockings up onto your legs. You release your breath slowly upon them, because they are made of such sheer, delicate material. How is such a miracle of fineness possible? You fear that even the gentlest touch might damage it.

Now the white shoes. No laces to tie, no

buckles. You simply step into these shoes, twisting your feet a little so that they fit. The shoes are almost large enough. Your feet are pinched, but not badly; it does not matter. Straightening, you glance at yourself in the mirror and see that you are suddenly taller—you are pressed forward, a fraction of an inch forward, and your hips are oddly raised.

Now the dress: It is made of white linen, fine linen, white enough and fine enough for a wedding dress. In fact, this is your wedding dress. You lift it cautiously, reverently, over your head. Must be very careful with the curls. . . . You make certain that the dress is unbuttoned, the pearl buttons undone all the way down, so that there will be plenty of room to pull the dress over your head. Slowly. Move slowly. You pause for an instant, thinking there is someone on the stairs—but you hear nothing— The door is locked and you are a stranger here in this secret room; there is nothing to fear. Anyway, there is no noise out on the stairs.

A rented room. A borrowed name.

The dress slides down over your head. Soft. Weightless. You open your eyes eagerly and find that you are staring at a young woman with an angular, bony, pale face, her eyes snatching at yours.

Hair flames about her head.

Her hands dart up to these curls, these coppery curls. They do not feel very soft—rather strawlike, artificial. But they look soft.

Now the buttons, which are very small. It takes several minutes to button them. You work painstakingly, without haste. It should be a pleasure to button this dress! Slowly, no hurry, no one is about to hammer upon the door and burst in upon you. You are absolutely alone.

And now the face. . . . The face must be applied with love. You have a small case with the necessary items, bought in a theatrical supply store. First you apply a liquid makeup that is called "Sunflower"; you smooth it carefully on your face and throat, using only upward strokes. Then you work on your eyes. This takes several minutes, because your hands are shaky and the mascara gets onto your lower eyelid. Then you outline your lips with a lipstick pencil and apply lipstick. The shade is "True Red." Finally you lift a box of loose powder and timidly pat a powder puff onto your skin. At first the effect is strange—too pale—ghostly—and then you even the powder out. Must work slowly, because a face is a work of art. Out on the street other people will glance at you, and your face must be a work of art.

Now.

You contemplate the young woman in the mirror.

The Secret Mirror

The descent to the street—the bustle of the noontime street—you walk with small, mincing steps, because your shoes are a little tight—your heart pounds with apprehension—your hands move up nervously to check the copper-colored hair, ah, the headband is so tight!—and now you hesitate at a curb, watching the traffic officer's baton—

The god of the baton.

Around you people have begun to stare. A child snickers. A woman smiles angrily at you, then her smile fades. Several men approach you. You begin to walk fast, back the way you have come. A sound behind you of footsteps—you look around in terror and see huge animals in the shapes of people pursuing you. You must run— the white shoes are painful, torturous—you want to kick them off but there is no time—the god of the crowd is nearly upon you—

You are the eye of a catastrophe that plummets through the city at noon, attracting stares on all sides, slowing traffic, causing the very clocks to pause— Someone jumps out of a doorway ahead of you. He is a fat-bellied man whose face shows that he is goodhearted and can recognize evil. His arms open wide for an embrace. You try to duck around him but it is too late— the first of the crowd has caught up with you— you feel yourself being mauled, shoved from hand to hand, your copper-colored hair torn from you

*in one instant with a laugh of derision, your
clothes torn from you, the stockings and the
garter belt flung up in the air—*

If you were a woman, the world would
rush at you now and penetrate you and deposit
in you, in the pit of your belly, a seed that would
flower into the world again, blossoming into the
world and renewing it. But you are not a woman
and the world cannot penetrate you. It can only
pound upon you with its fists and kick at you
and shout into your face with a hearty furious
derision.

So you will not go down to the street after
all.

It is noontime. There would be danger out
on the street. You stand before your secret mirror
for a long time—for fifteen, twenty minutes—
hypnotized by that reflection. It is a woman who
stares back at you with watery eyes. Her mouth
quivers beneath its perfect red shape.

You remove the curls with your own hands,
beginning to weep. At once the reflection in the
mirror begins to weep. You are both weeping for
your lost selves, whom no one can return to you,
but who have slipped out of the mirror now,
untouched, unpursued.

The Cruel Master

✦

The Master, at first not understood to be cruel, called Dr. Thomaz to him one evening in February.

Dr. Thomaz, fifty-six, of moderate height with fine, severe, rather ashen skin, who was seen in the rainy winter months wearing a dark overcoat with wide, old-fashioned lapels and a large gray hat set square upon his head, had been known in the city for decades because of his services for the government on matters of public health.

On February 15, he attended the wedding of his favorite nephew, a young man of twenty-nine. Dr. Thomaz, though forcing himself to

attend to the familiar services out of considera-
tion for his family and affection for his nephew,
found himself growing restless and tired in church.
His head seemed to grow heavy, as if swelling.

Afterward, the young nephew, fair-skinned
and taller than Dr. Thomaz, accepted Dr.
Thomaz's congratulations, smiling down into his
face with a strange reckless glow, as if he were
not seeing Dr. Thomaz but looking through his
face to someone else. Dr. Thomaz understood
that his nephew was excited, and forgave him.

Strangely exhausted, almost frightened at his
weariness, Dr. Thomaz excused himself early. He
drove home at once, had the car put away, and
hurried to his study on the first floor of his town
house, where he lay down on his black leather
sofa. His head felt enlarged with exhaustion. He
did not recall having felt so tired in the past, and
he feared becoming ill, because illness would
keep him from his work.

It's only because of that wedding, he thought.
A wedding is a curse.

This thought surprised him, because he did
not believe it. It was not a thought he had created
himself. No, he did not believe it. But now he
was lying on the sofa, completely alone in the
house except for one of the servants, who would
not bother him, and he felt so tired that he could
not have moved if he had desired to move—so
the thought held him prisoner, as if whispered

into his ear by someone else, paralyzing him for several seconds as it seemed to float in his unresisting brain.

When the thought had faded away, Dr. Thomaz was asleep.

He dreamed. He was walking briskly up the wide, handsome cobblestone walk of a country house. It was no longer February; judging from the roses and the fig trees, it must have been midsummer. At first Dr. Thomaz thought the estate looked familiar, then he realized he had never seen it before. He did not recognize the coat of arms on the cornice of the house. This disturbed him, but his energetic, brisk walk did not falter, as if it belonged to another person.

The house was made of granite that had darkened. It was immense and not very attractive. A number of iron-railed verandas—as many as fifteen, Dr. Thomaz calculated dizzily—protruded from the façade of the house, giving a heavy, turgid look to the architecture. On either side of the broad pathway were rows of chestnut trees, magnificent trees, but their lower branches had been allowed to grow at will. Just before the main entrance of the house was a marble pool in which dark, dank water had gathered, and a thick yellowing layer of leaves. Flies and small mosquitoes buzzed languidly; Dr. Thomaz waved a mosquito away from his face. The odor of manure and earth was rich in the air.

He stood now before the portal. Everything was silent. His heartbeat quickened with anticipation of the appointment he had within the house . . . but there was no one around, no human movement. Who was the Master here? Would he appear in another moment to shake Dr. Thomaz's trembling hand?

Silence. Dr. Thomaz entered the house. His face, with a peculiar elasticity he had not experienced for decades—since the years of his early manhood—prepared itself to smile in greeting. But no one approached. The Master of the house awaited him, but in another room. Dr. Thomaz went immediately to the wide staircase and ascended the stairs to the second floor. The house was dim and unclear to him, as if out of focus or not fully imagined. He had a vague impression of furniture draped in white.

He entered a room whose patterned marble flooring was dingy with age. The room was nearly unfurnished. At the far end of the room a window was open and Dr. Thomaz understood that he was to approach this window. He felt a sense of alarm, sudden terror. He looked behind him but saw no one—nor was anyone waiting in this room, which was obviously prepared for him, being so empty and so still. Dr. Thomaz did not want to approach the window; his eyes felt strained, bulging, as if a tremendous sucking pressure in the air were drawing them out. He would not look, no! The Master could not force him to look!

He went to the window and stared out. There, in a courtyard, was a figure, a boy harnessing a horse to a cart; he was scolding the horse and seemed to have no awareness of Dr. Thomaz. A young peasant boy, with a thick head of dark blond hair, a confusion of curls that the humid air had made fuzzy. . . . Dr. Thomaz stood, staring, his lips dry and drawn back from his teeth. He wanted to turn away from the window, but he could not move. And at that moment the boy shrieked, in surprise and pain. The horse had thrust at him with its forelegs. The horse, gone wild, knocked the boy backward and tried to trample him. The boy was shrieking, he had evidently suffered a broken arm, since Dr. Thomaz could see, quite clearly, the white bone jutting through his tannd skin. . . .

He woke. A convulsive shiver woke him. He was lying on the leather couch and it was very late; confused, he looked about him and could not at first recall what he was doing in his study. After a few minutes he rose shakily and walked about the room, touching the familiar objects. He poured a drink and drank it, not sitting down. It was good to feel his feet so solidly against the floor and to know he was no longer dreaming.

Yet his head felt ravaged, his eyes felt still the strain of that pressure. He decided not to

attempt sleep any more that night. He had work
to do which might distract him—a pile of some
ten or twelve medical journals to read in various
languages—letters he must write to colleagues—
He was afraid to sleep any more.

He drove to the hospital at dawn, but once
in his office suite he felt too tired to work. He
did not trust himself with work in this condition.
So he told one of the young nurses he was going
to rest, and he lay down on a cot in a room
adjoining his office, pleased at the silence of this
place, the dim white walls and white floor.

The Master pronounced his name: the name
hung suspended in Dr. Thomaz's brain. Then, as
it faded, Dr. Thomaz found himself back in that
room again, but this time he was lying on a small
bed—a cot like the one at the hospital—and he
stared at the several items in the room, which
had obviously been brought in for his benefit.
In addition to the cot was a small, squat table
with a pitcher of water on it, an old, chipped
porcelain bowl, and a pile of some three or four
white towels. As if to soften the terror Dr. Thomaz
must feel, the cot was made up with the same
thick, heavily starched sheets that were used at
the hospital.

He got to his feet cautiously. Again the
window was open. Again he knew he must go
to it. He could already hear the horse's desperate,
angry whinnying. With his hand pressed against

his heart, as if to protect it from the dizzying vibrations of the horse's screams, he approached the window. There, down in the courtyard, the young boy was struggling to harness the horse again. This time the horse appeared larger; its dark brown coat gleamed with strength. Its eyes rolled madly. The boy was shouting at it—a word Dr. Thomaz could not make out—and if Dr. Thomaz had called out a warning, the boy would not have heard it.

A small cloud of enormous horseflies, glinting blue-black in the sun, hovered around the window sill. The odor of manure was very strong here. Dr. Thomaz leaned out the window, staring in silence, as the boy wrestled with the horse—leaping up to bring its head down, down brutally —and he saw that the boy's shoulders were wiry and muscular, but his hands were rather small, his feet rather small. He wanted to shout a warning to the boy. What if the horse turns viciously upon him, what if the boy's arm is broken . . . ? Dr. Thomaz had forgotten all he knew as a doctor; so far out in the country here, rushed into mid-summer out of a cold drizzling winter, he would not be able to help, but would simply hang out the window, gaping like a fool.

The sudden shriek again. The boy's body tossed down, bone showing through the flesh, the opaque flesh of the horse's white, blind eyes. The boy's face a mask of pain, incredible surprise.

Dr. Thomaz wished to hide his own face and turn away from this sight, but the Master of the house held him still. He could not move. *You are a doctor in attendance here and you cannot run away*, Dr. Thomaz found himself thinking.

He woke with this thought held clearly in his mind: then, as he came to his senses, agitated, baffled, the thought slowly faded.

He woke. He had been sleeping at the hospital, and now it was late afternoon. Late afternoon! He got to his feet, stunned. He had already missed an appointment . . . several appointments. . . . He went to take a shower. He washed himself hurriedly, smelling the odor of manure on his own body. He believed he could hear, muffled by the water's splashing, the shrieks and groans of the boy. . . . Afterward, dressed, his damp hair carefully combed, he crossed the walk to another part of the hospital and saw at a distance a young girl in the company of a nun. The girl's faltering steps and her plaited blond hair made him think immediately of the young peasant in his dream, so cruelly abused. . . .

His sleep had not refreshed him; his head ached with weariness. But the thought of sleep disturbed him and he wondered if he would ever be able to sleep again. To surrender himself to sleep, what a risk! He would return to that room again. He would approach the window again, helplessly. He would hear a breathing not his own, he would sense a heartbeat in the air. The presence of another person, close to him, breathing along with him, his heartbeat perfectly timed to coincide with his. . . . And he would want to cry out in revulsion against the cruel Master who had brought him to this place: *Who are you? Why do you torture the boy?* But he would be unable to speak.

That evening he visited his mother and, while she was engaged in a long, querulous conversation with her cook on the subject of fish soups, he wandered out of the old woman's sitting room—which smelled faintly of illness, for his mother had not been well for years—and approached the kitchen. He never entered the kitchen here, or in his own home, but as a child he had often wandered through the dark, cavernous room, and now he wondered what he might find there. He recalled flies buzzing there, years ago. . . . But, at the kitchen door, he paused and came to his senses and returned to his mother's room. He was a little giddy with exhaustion. He listened politely to his mother's small whining speeches and felt a sensation of nausea, not because of what his mother was saying, but because of the fact of her words, the fact that she was speaking. She was a very small, withered woman, and Dr. Thomaz thought that he would like to slip sideways through her words, like a playing card, thin as a playing card. When the cook replied, he felt suddenly, keenly, that he was in danger of slipping sideways through the words of these old women: he must force himself to his senses.

His mother scolded him for looking so tired. She told him to go home and sleep.

And he drove home at once, following her instructions, his heartbeat already pounding. He must sleep, yes, he must risk sleep again. . . . But as soon as he lay down he seemed to be waking again in that room, sitting up in confusion. How quickly he had moved from his mother's house to this stranger's house, where the Master remained always out of sight! For a few seconds he could not move. He recalled the summer he had had to wear a cast on his leg, as a child of six, and the fear, the heat, the sense of being punished rushed back to him. He began to cry as a child might cry. Hot, stinging tears. The Master might be standing outside the door of his room, listening. He might call out in contempt, *Why are you crying? Did I bring you here to turn into a child of six?*

Dr. Thomaz hurried to the window. Evidently he was ahead of time, for he saw the boy leading the horse out of a barn without any difficulty, headed for the spot in the courtyard just beneath the window. The cart had nothing on it, it was like a stage prop. The horse was not so striking as Dr. Thomaz remembered, and it seemed bemused and groggy, as if just awakened. It tossed its head once, preparing to take its place in this story.

Dr. Thomaz, perspiring, waited helplessly for the boy to begin the struggle. The boy tugged at the horse's bridle. He yelled out something at the horse. The horse began to rear in a frenzy. Dr. Thomaz was going to shout *No, no*, at the crucial moment, but his throat seemed to close, and the boy fell backward with a shriek. . . . The shriek sounded more surprised than before, like an animal's shriek. This time the horse came down with both forelegs on the boy's back just as the boy rolled over, and Dr. Thomaz heard a thud that was sickening . . . he stared down at the exposed bone, saw the bright flood of red about the boy's mouth and nose. . . .

He sat up, awake. Awake in his own bedroom. His heart pounded with excitement and he understood that he must lie back again, soothing himself, he must fall asleep again. The Master demanded this. He feared sleep and yet he must force himself to sleep. It was expected. *Infinite patterns exist in sleep*, he thought, *but only one pattern when I am awake*.

He was fearful, yet he forced himself to lie back again. He closed his eyes. A pulse began to beat in his mind, powerfully, straining the eyeballs. He waited. Then he found himself slipping into that other room, like a shadow gliding along

a stone wall, and he was at the window again
with his hand pressed against his heart, staring
at the boy and the horse. He had arrived just
at the instant when the horse slashed at the boy,
knocking him backward. Ah, it was happening!
It had happened, and now the boy rolled over
as if to protect his face and stomach, already
screaming, a torrent of blood flowing from his
mouth and nose. . . . Dr. Thomaz leaned out
the window, anxious to see everything. He was
anxious that the boy should shriek even more
loudly than before, and that the horse should
whinny in that vicious, choking manner. Now the
horse came down upon the boy, its hoofs solid
and slipping on his soft body. . . . A small faint
cloud of flies buzzed around this scene.

Dr. Thomaz, panting, looked down upon
the body that lay beneath his window and could
find no words to utter. The cart had been knocked
awry. It was an odd cart, much too small to be
harnessed to the horse. The horse itself had
broken away and now was wandering off to graze,
in absolute silence.

It was over.

And now? Now Dr. Thomaz must escape.
He could do nothing for that bleeding, broken
body, he must escape. He could not stop the
hemorrhaging from the boy's mouth and nose.

He hurried out of the room and down the
stairs and outside, he hurried along the broad

pathway lined with chestnut trees gone wild, willing to hurry, to run. He was late. He would be missed back in Lisbon. Out on the highway he walked fast, on his way home. He willed himself to wake up: to wake suddenly in his own bed. But he could not wake up. The dream usually ended before this, but now it had not ended and he was sentenced to a long walk home. He laughed aloud in his nervousness. Why didn't the dream end and release him? What use had the dream for him now?

The road was not like the road of a dream. It was not misty and insubstantial; it was an ordinary road. There was nothing sinister or memorable about it. The sky, fixed in an ordinary pattern of cloud, was not sinister in any way, nor was it memorable: this fact alarmed Dr. Thomaz. If he was not dreaming, then he would not be able to wake. He would be forced to think about the boy in the courtyard, who was perhaps dying at this very moment, blood rushing from his smashed face.... There was nothing Dr. Thomaz could do for him now. The country road was empty and no one was watching him. The Master, whose presence had been so strong back at the house, was now withdrawing, leaving Dr. Thomaz to utter freedom.

If he had everything to re-live, he would not change a moment. Not a single moment. Not the boy's struggle, not his shrieks, his being thrown so heavily to the ground! How vivid that scene was, how unforgettable! Dr. Thomaz had never witnessed anything like it. For all his adult life he had cared for the sick and the injured, wrestling with them, but now, with a beating heart that seemed concentrated on the roof of his parched mouth, he was free to simply contemplate the fact of their suffering.

Many hours later he found himself on the outskirts of the city. He was able to make his way home near dawn, shivering with the cold of a perpetual drizzling rain, his overcoat collar turned up about his neck and his hat on his head soaked. He approached his home, where everyone was sleeping. He himself was sleeping there. He stood on the sidewalk and stared at the house, which he had rarely seen from this point of view at this time of day, standing outside by himself, afraid to enter. He could not bring himself to move. He could not go to the door and let himself in, could not hurry upstairs to his bedroom. . . . There, in that bedroom, he himself was still sleeping; he did not dare force himself upon that scene. . . .

He stood in the street, unable to move. He would have to await the Master in order that things be made right again. A mistake had occurred. Only the Master could correct it. Yet Dr. Thomaz thought the Master, who was nowhere near, might not care to correct the mistake. It had been Dr. Thomaz's mistake, not the Master's. And a further problem: the Master had only been hypothesized, by Dr. Thomaz himself. He had never seen the Master face to face and could not prove that he existed.

He had had knowledge of only two individuals, himself and the boy in the courtyard. Between the two there was perhaps a necessary relationship that involved a third person. . . . But Dr. Thomaz had never looked upon this third person and would not know how to beg his life from him if he had.

He stood in the street, in the rain, waiting for the Master to call him back.

Sunlight / Twilight

❧❦❧

Sunlight. A heavy book rests in your lap. You are sitting in the courtyard of your country home, and behind you in the enormous house people glance out at you occasionally, spying on you.

He is sitting quietly. He is sitting quietly in the sunlight.

The pages of this old book are puckered. An odor of darkness and dampness lifts to your nostrils. You turn the pages of the book slowly, unhurriedly. The book is completed; the epoch in history that it describes has been over for hundreds of years. There are colored plates protected by tissue paper, torn in places . . . perhaps you tore it as a child, accidentally, or impatiently . . . ?

You know this book, you know how it ends. The colored plates of ancient armies. Gladiators. Spears held proudly erect, men with sinewy thighs, calves, bodies wrapped in leather, breastplates strapped to their enormous torsos. Streams of blood flowing down bare chests.

". . . a little soup?"

Ana stands there, her solid face perched stiffly upon her neck, her solid body stiffly before you. Staring. Her small eyes. Your mother has sent her out and she has obeyed.

"No, thank you," you whisper.

Your mouth twists with fear of her, of those small eyes.

How long must you wait until they all die and no one remembers?

You close your eyes suddenly because the sunlight is so strong. And immediately you are patroling the street, "patroling" that certain street as you did in October and November, whistling through your teeth and your parched lips. . . . Ah, yes, that certain street! There it is! *He is sitting quietly*, Ana will tell your mother.

You are twenty years old. A thin, elongated body, shoulders slightly stooped to minimize your height, a head carried assertively, pushed out and up from those shoulders. Eyes that blink slowly, baffled as if by light or noise. Your boyhood is still in your face.

Someone approaches you. Your mother. *Hello! Isn't the sunlight warm!* You stare at your mother's stern, pale, ravaged face, dreading her words.

"Hello! Isn't the sunlight pleasant!" she cries.

You stammer a reply.

She sits near you. Has brought out a French news mazagine. It is not a magazine she usually reads; it is to interest you, maybe.

She has just returned from the eleven-o'clock Mass. You have gone with her only once since coming to the country. Too much pain there in the chapel, the twilight. Kneeling. The need to pray with hands lifted to hide your face, fingers groping against your own face. Your mother goes to Mass twice a day and there she prays for you, her eyes shut tight, her large, broad hands, hidden by gloves, lifted to her face.

Her shadow is now motionless on the grass, near you. Your head rings, reels. If you dare to close your eyes you are immediately in the city again, prowling the city. The wet dusk of a November evening. Not in the sunlight. You are hurrying down some stone steps, plunging steeply down . . . a puddle at the bottom, a water puddle in which half-rotted leaves float. . . . You walk with your collar turned smartly up, like a man in an American movie.

Your mother is speaking. Far away, speaking. Yes, she is speaking of your oldest brother, who is still in Rome. . . . You try to listen but you are back in the street, in the twilight, hurrying, desperate to get somewhere. . . . An appointment? The cold choking sensation in your chest: a desperate evening.

Knocking at a door. Bare knuckles. Your labored breath.

A heavyset woman opens the door—stares at you.

"He isn't home. Go away," she says.

You understand that he is not home because the air from the house feels thinner, a disappointment—if H were at home, the air would seep outward with his warmth, his size.

You go away.

Your mother has said something. You open your eyes and try to smile, blinking.

"Are you ill?" she whispers.

No. No.

She contemplates you, weighs you. Does not reach out to touch you. After a moment she says, as if nothing were wrong, "Your father will be home this weekend. He's definite about that."

Your father has not been out here for weeks. He saw you at the hospital: lifted the covers before anyone could stop him, saw what they had done to you.

"That will be nice," you say.

Lifted the covers before anyone could stop him.

You turn the pages of the book in order to escape from your mother's stare. She must not stare at you like that. Must not stare. There was a great deal of blood: it splattered in surprise.

"That old book is so heavy for you to carry around, and so dusty . . ." your mother says in dismay.

She will pick at you like the dullest knife. The dull tarnished blade of a knife. A cheap knife, an insult of a knife. She will pick at you.

You are wearing clothes that are too warm for this spring day. Your shoes are like boots. You are buttoned up and zipped up. No part of you can hang out. No part of you except your hands and your neck and your head is exposed.

Mother wants to ask if you are ill. Wants to ask what you are thinking about.

Close your eyes and you see the gang of boys—see yourself hurrying to them. Ah, you are ungainly even in your handsome black coat!— you try to shorten yourself. Shoulders sloping, head thrust forward from the neck, like a bird. H approaches you with a whoop of a greeting. Is he joking?—laughing at you? Or glad to see you? The boys suck at cigarettes the way men in movies suck at cigarettes.

H is wearing the wristwatch. There it is: the gold bracelet strains around his thick wrist.

The boys keep glancing at one another. Faces keep twitching with secrets. They have something to show you, they say. An alley, very narrow, through which you all pass in silence, except for one of the boys, who giggles . . . a short swarthy fellow with shining eyes. His grin seeks you out and you smile in turn, smiling with him. You sink deeper and deeper into that smile, into that alley, into the twilight.

An old shed. Sloped roof. You want to declare that you must be somewhere else, you want to turn and walk away. They are only boys, fifteen and sixteen years old. Ignorant, poor, swarming like animals. You do not like these boys.

But you don't walk away.

Mother is saying, ". . . in the house and have lunch and then a nap? Wouldn't that be a good idea?"

You say nothing, turning the pages of the book. The book has an ornate binding. Letters in gold, nearly worn away. It has been in the family for two hundred years. When you were in the hospital you requested this book, remembering it exactly, but they didn't bring it to you. As soon as you were brought here you got the book from the old library and began reading it as if there were something here you must understand.

The Moors . . . the invasions . . . the crumbling castles and the splashes of blood. . . .

You must have agreed with Mother, for now the two of you are walking up to the house. She carries both your book and her magazine. You are walking stiffly, carefully. The pain at the pit of your belly is exaggerated by your mother's presence, which exaggerates everything.

In the dark foyer you are confused for an instant—your mind jumps—you seem to be entering another dark place, groping for support. Your skin is exposed. You can't stop shivering. You are naked. You are beginning to whimper, to cry: Why are you hiding? Why is it dark? Why doesn't H put out his hand and say this is a joke?

Better for him if he had bled to death, your father told the doctor.

You tried to bleed to death. Yes, but your body dragged you out to the street. White naked convulsing body in the street, in the rain. The eruption of blood. You tried to hold yourself together, fit the parts back together.

You will never tell them H's name. Never think of his full name any longer, for fear you may speak it out loud.

Large bowls of soup. Are you expected to eat all that soup? You stare into the milky watery substance and your mouth locks itself into a grin.

Mother is watching.

This table slants in one direction—back to him, to H. To the boys and their sniggering mouths. To the watch H wore so proudly, though he never thanked you for it. The shed, the round of faces, the matches snapped to flames—H with his knife and his nervous giggle. *We are going to fix you up,* they cried. Drunk from wine. Only boys, a few years younger than you.

What if Mother asks you suddenly, "Why do you dream about them? About *him*? Why does the table tilt in his direction, why to him and not to me? Why do you cower in your sleep, calling to him and shrinking from him?"

Your fingers have seized the soup spoon but you cannot eat. You sit in silence. You are stammering words in silence. *Everything tilts downhill to him,* you want to explain. *It runs from you, whom I do not love, to him, whom I love.*

In spite of your pain and your sorrow, you understand that the world is put together perfectly.

Husband and Wife

❦

. . . . lie down in tenderness, his arms embracing and releasing her, gently, relinquishing her to the night. He seems very tired. Sun-exhausted, still warm from the long hours of sun; he murmurs that his eyeballs feel seared. It is a country of radiance. He falls asleep and she remains awake, feeling the warmth of his body, as if the sunlight were still shining upon it.

. . . . she thinks of herself as a woman lying awake beside a man in the dark. But the *dark* is not really dark. There is a dim, iridescent light in the room, an intense shadow. The objects of the room are not clearly defined but they do not blend simply into one another.

. . . . He is asleep already. His breath has become heavy, labored, irregular. His face is a small planet turned toward her. She sees his face dimly, but clearly; only the blackest of nights could hide that face from her. He sighs, he must be dreaming, his lips twitch as if in a fearful smile. His eyes are shadows, the hollows of a moon. She lies very still, watching him. If she were to put her hand out to touch him, to touch that warm aggressive flesh, she would feel the ribs beneath the sturdy skin like ribs of sand beneath small unhurried waves.

. . . . asleep, dreaming, distant from her, his face seems to rear up out of an element like water, nudging her. But he does not move. She stares at him from a distance of inches. Her throat closes involuntarily, as if she were in the presence of something mysterious and frightful.

. . . . His face has become slightly distorted, due to the heaviness of his sleep. There is a density about him, a demanding tension. He is a warlike planet. A slight acrid smell of war about him, like a vapor. Her mind races with a sudden bewilderment, a sudden fear. She is awake and cannot sleep and is a witness to him as he changes into sleep. As if he senses her agitation, he turns suddenly away. A small shaking of the earth. The mattress strains, creaks.

. . . . Time passes and she yearns to put her arms around him, to comfort him in his quarrel, his struggle. *What is he destroying?* She does not dare move. The back of his head is dark, his hair is very dark, like a blot of pure darkness against the pillow. A shape of darkness, with a faint acrid smell she does not recognize. She smiles suddenly in fear, against her will, and senses her own teeth glimmering overwhite in the darkness, like teeth in an overexposed photograph.

. . . . His muscles tense and shrug beneath the cover. He is arguing with someone, about to lunge forward to someone. Straining in his sleep as if trudging uphill, stumbling on curbs, stairs. A kind of exclamation is garbled, kept down inside his throat. He has recognized someone.

. . . . Unable to sleep, she lies beside him, stiff, not wanting to hear him, not that hoarse angry breathing or the choked words, not wanting to feel the jerks and lunges of his muscles. Her own body has become tamed and curious and light, as his has become heavy. She is like a body carried along by the current of the river. A mysterious body, unclaimed, not quite recognized by those on shore. The other morning she stared out at the river: yes, there something was floating, a dark shape floating, yes, like a body. The size of a body. Distances on the water are confusing but, yes, she believed that was a body, a human body; a cold fear ran through her as she knew with certainty that it was a body, a corpse. . . . It had turned slowly, idly in the river, in the sunshine, carried along by the waves, unhurried, without sex or age, a body that did not show its face to her, the shape of a body pressing upon her eyelids as she closed them in panic, in shame.

. . . . She told no one about the body in the river.

. . . . The floating body, the floating shape of a body, had turned gently in the water and did not reveal itself to her. No, it had no face. It was far away and she could not be certain it was a human body. At that time her husband had been gone from home, in the city, and she had felt his body holding her back, preventing her from running to the riverbank. Her husband was a small constant weight that held her down, back, away from the riverbank, so that she stood in a buzzing of fear that was somehow safe, not fearful, while the shape of the body was carried away downstream. Later, when her husband came home, she told him nothing about the body in the river.

. . . . Her husband turns again, suddenly. She draws back so he will not touch her. One of his hands appears beside his face. On the pillow beside his face, the way a child might sleep. His hand is distorted because it is so close to her eyes, it is a shadow with the rough stern edges of a shovel, held up as if to block out her vision or to threaten her. It rises out of a columnar shape, an arm.

. . . . His hand is like a shovel or an oar or a weapon. *I want to be somewhere else*, she thinks suddenly. These words surprise her because they are not her words. She wants to wake her husband, she wants only to embrace him in love, but she fears disturbing his sleep. She fears something about him. *I want to be somewhere else*. No, she wants only to be here, she wants only to embrace him because his sleep is so disturbing. Sometimes in the day he walks with his head raised, expectant, tense, as if waiting to hear a voice out of the air calling him by name —pronouncing his name absolutely—he can dream back centuries, to an army of ancestors, noblemen with faces he must imagine as being his own. She fears waking him now because he might slash out at her, mistaking her for one of his fathers.

. . . . The room is a garden, though darkened. If she were to turn on the light she would see the intricate dull green and peacock green and soft gold designs in the wall, the designs of a garden. There, along the molding at the ceiling, are ferns and ornate designs that seem both paper and green flesh, the flesh of plants. The *trompe-l'oeil* ceiling leads back into a real garden with a temple. Figures move lightly in the background, the women in ancient stiff dresses, their faces too small to be seen. They are shading their eyes, though there is no sun. They are staring out at a silvery river that runs through their world, marred with ripples, shadowy shapes, shapes of the river's current itself or perhaps the shapes of strangers' bodies, strangers' corpses. These women do not glance down into the room, where a man lies sleeping beside a woman.

. . . . The river in the ceiling runs through the smallest capillaries of the woman, who cannot sleep. She lies stiffly beside her husband. She feels the hot charge of his desire through the river of her blood, but his desire is urgent, tense, impersonal, a stranger's desire, not for her. He stirs, grinds his teeth. His hand closes into a fist. She feels his sudden emotion and would like to flee from it: so vicious a river, so vicious a pressure of fluid, should be cut off at its source.

. . . . His sigh is deep, wracking, as if he were clearing his chest of an old grief. His hand moves toward her. Brushes against her face, gropes to her shoulder . . . takes hold of her shoulder. . . . There is a strength in his fingers, but it is a strength of neutrality. It does not recognize her. Now he is muttering something she cannot understand. He shakes her a little. She is silent, staring at him. She thinks that he will wake before he hurts her. He will wake and recognize her. But he shakes her again and now presses her back onto the bed, muttering something. An argument, anger that is baffled and drawn out, as if ancient anger, a rehearsal of anger, out of his control. *I want to be something else,* a voice in her brain cries, but it is not her voice. Her husband rears up over her suddenly, presses himself down upon her, his mouth grinding hotly against the side of her face, his words do not come to the surface and she hears only that muttering, that drawn-out groan. . . .

. . . . His knees, his thighs drive her legs apart. No resistance in her. He does not expect any resistance—his thighs do not expect any resistance—and she lies beneath him, not daring to move. A stranger has thrown his arm across her, has taken hold of her, has lowered his heavy body upon hers, and now he drives her legs apart, open, he has begun to jab at her and she does not dare move. He does not know her. Does not call her by name. He jabs at her body, which has tightened out of fear. She feels how over-white her teeth have become, and sharp as the teeth of a small perfect saw. To be sawed side-ways gently, neatly, against the flesh of this stranger's throat, with a pressure that does not relent until the soft, tough skin breaks. . . .

. . . . But then he falls from her, seems to fall from her body as if down a small height. Pushes her from him, as if he has used her up. He lies on his side, sleeping, heavy, unconscious, in a kind of stupor. He murmurs, *Ask her—that one—ask her—her—Forgive—Forgive me—*

. . . . The night breaks in two. Two parts. The old night leans away into darkness; the new night leans toward morning, it is lighter, thinner. She is still sleepless but she feels her bloodbeat re-turning to her. It is over. The danger is over. It has risen in him, hotly and fiercely, but nothing has happened and she is safe, he is still sleeping, his sleep is quieter now. She can remember the heaviness of his body, its thrusting at her . . . but the memory seems to belong to another night, to another woman. She draws her hand slowly across her face and seems to be erasing this memory.

. . . . He sleeps almost silently now. She watches him in the lightening dark and sees that his mouth is now closed, his lips pursed, he is breathing peacefully, almost silently. His breath is regular. His profile, against the shadowy jumble of a cabinet and a wall, is familiar and peaceful in sleep. She would like to embrace him, to forgive him, but she does not want to disturb his sleep. Her heartbeat has slowed, slowed. She is now on the edge of sleep herself.

. . . . Tenderly she sleeps, relinquishing herself to sleep. Now his body and hers seem the same body, the two of them rocking gently in a kind of sac held under water, held under sleep. She sighs, releasing her soul to the air . . . she falls asleep upon a thought of her husband, a thought of her perfect love for him. . . . There is an iridescence to the room: their damp, drying skin, the sheen of the wallpaper, the miniature faces in the ceiling, the inch-long shapes in that satiny river overhead, the shapes of bodies not brought into focus.

The Poisoned Kiss

Not one hundred yards from my courtyard the first stranger lurched in front of me—it was necessary for me to shove him aside. He stumbled back against a wall firm and weathered with the centuries, too surprised to cry out after me. I hurried on toward you.

Again someone blundered in front of me— my precious pathway to you!—and I seized him by the arm, shook him viciously, tried to thrust him aside. But he struggled. It was necessary for me to close my fingers about his throat. He fell to his knees, choking, and I rushed past.

And again, as I ran through the tumbled-down cloister, scattering the old bones about me in my haste to you, a sight-seer approached me and tried to detain me with idle questions. Blood rushed into my eyes—my vision was nearly obliterated—I was led by my rage to shout into this fool's face and beat him away from me. He persisted. There was an open tomb in which some whole bones lay in the midst of dust and rubble; I took hold of this fool and, with a strength I did not know I possessed, forced him down into the tomb.

Did he choke in all that dust?

Running, soaring to you—to your kiss—I dream with my bloodied eyes wide open, dreaming of your arms and your slender neck and your white, white skin, your laughter delicate as a thrush's song, your eyes so darkly lidded, so beautiful. I dream again and again of your kiss.

Why do they insist upon approaching me, touching me? blocking my way? Why do they address the most absurd questions to me, as if I were a mere stroller with no destination, a gentleman on a Sunday afternoon with no one awaiting him? As soon as they see my face darkened by the blood of my anger, they understand—but by then it is too late.

I have acquired a small, sharp dagger.

The ground between you and me is uncertain, and as I run it cracks and threatens to split. So I must run faster. I run soaring over the deepening cracks, and behind me there are gaps in the earth into which other men have fallen, weeping in agony.

The Son of God
and His Sorrow

⁂

I was born in a northern village on the windy
edge of the sea, near the Lima River.

My father was a fisherman who died when
I was three years old. My mother carried me
everywhere with her and was always whispering
to me, telling me stories of my future: that I
would never go out to sea like my father, but
would subdue the waves from the shore. I would
make the waters still enough for men to walk
upon.

My mother's mother stared at me. "He has

a face of such purity . . ." she would whisper.

When I was a small child I already felt the strangeness of my divinity: a face so comely and bright that neighbors would stare at me, their eyes snagging in mine so that I had to turn away, ashamed.

I grew ashamed of my own beauty.

A woman joked coarsely with my mother: that I belonged to the nobleman in the castle on a hill to the north of the village. My mother, who had grown very thin and reckless over the years, her eyes staring straight at you with their stiff, black lashes rarely blinking, laughed angrily and did not reply. There was no nobleman in the castle now. All the family had gone away and only servants lived there, brothers and sisters and cousins of our villagers. The castle had granite walls fortified by six square towers; it had been built many centuries ago, no one knows how long, and the first king visited in it, so people said.

The priest of our village looked with fondness upon me and blessed me. He was a man much older than my mother, with harsh grizzled hair and one eye that did not focus right.

He taught me the response of the Mass when I was very young. He marveled at my ability to remember the strange words. Along with several older boys I assisted him at the

Sacrifice of the Mass until I was eight years old. Then, one morning in winter, I could no longer bear to hear him speaking those sacred words, and a kind of convulsion overcame me. I stumbled down from the altar and crouched in a dark corner of the church, my hands pressed over my ears.

The priest tried to make me stand, and his touch was poisonous on my skin. But I would not move. Finally my mother came, weeping, and took me away.

I lay in a fever for ten days.

While this sickness burned in me, God spoke to me for the first time. His voice was mixed up with the priest's questioning voice and with the voices of my relatives. Then their voices faded and I could hear only the voice of God, burning in me, telling me I could not hide any longer. I brought my fingers up to my eyes and peered through them at my mother's haggard face. *You cannot hide any longer.*

The priest came again and his presence was an outrage to me. I screamed and put my hands over my eyes.

From that time until now I have wandered, at first in the north, then down along the seacoast, and everywhere I go people await me. Sometimes I draw back shyly when I see them. Sometimes I hurry to them, knowing that they need me. In the most mocking of faces there is a pause, a fearful hesitation, and then the face changes as I am recognized. I shun churches and places that are believed to be holy, knowing they are not holy, but I do not speak out against them.

I speak to my father, God, and God speaks to me, simply, in a language all can understand. God uses my own voice to speak to me. I reply in my own voice. We do not always agree. We are very close, living close together as if He is in my pocket and I am in His pocket, our elbows bumping, our hair brushing each other's mouth. Sometimes I feel the tingling of His impatience; He, larger than I and centuries older, sometimes must feel the nervous horselike energy of my young body.

On a late summer day, in the Beira Alta, we had our most serious argument. A young boy had been injured while working in a field. I was brought to him and knelt alongside him and kissed the ugly wound on his forehead. God chose this time to speak sharply to me: *You are wanted elsewhere, fifty miles from here! You must leave!* But I did not leave the child. I bowed down low to the ground while in a circle around us people stood weeping and muttering and praying. God recoiled from me in anger.

I lifted the boy in my arms and carried him into the village.

Everyone followed me. It was late in the

summer and the summer had been very dry. Now great dust clouds floated away toward the mountains in the shapes of animals and fish. There was a terrible hot smell to the land. People noticed the strange shapes but said nothing. The boy's father kept clutching at me and begging me to save his son. Blood flowed down into the dirt and formed precious beads; the boy's blood flowed onto me. All was silent. Even the oxen stared at our procession and did not shrug their bodies and make their yokes creak. We felt how God stared angrily at us and was choosing His words carefully.

When He spoke again, it was out of my mouth: *You will not disobey me. You are wanted fifty miles from here, where a woman has fallen into a deep pool and cannot be revived*—I did not reply. Trembling, I lay the boy down in his father's bed and knelt beside him. I whispered to him: *You will wake up, you will look around at all of us in amazement and remember nothing that has happened this afternoon.* Many people were crowded into the room. My master retreated to the highest peak of the roof and glared down at us, so that the back of my neck burned with His rage. But I did not abandon the boy. In a few minutes he opened his eyes. He was an ugly child with a blemished, discolored face. He gaped at so many people standing around him and sat up and tried to get to his feet, while his mother cried out in joy and embraced him.

You are the Son of God! The Son of God! the people cried at me.

Now God rushed back to me. *You must leave this village,* He muttered, and I got at once to my feet and hurried out of the stone house, though everyone tried to hold me back. *Now you will fly along the road, you will cross the mountain as lightly as a flurry of dust—* My breath came in jagged pants as I flew along the rocky land, the villagers' voices fading behind me, their joy merging with the monotonous rhythm of the wind. In a swirl of dust I arrived in the other village. Tears flooded my eyes from the flight through the dusty air and my face shone bright as a flame. People who looked upon me cried out. They hid their faces, crossed themselves, peered through their fingers at me.

God directed me to the bank of the pool where the woman lay. I fell upon her dizzily and brought her back to life. She sat up as the child had sat up, and vomited into her hands.

For months after that God and I meditated upon the nature of our argument. He said that I was His son and must obey. He said that I must never go against His word. I said that a small fury had risen in me and had acted in my place, not as the Son of God but as someone else. He said this must never happen again. I promised it would never happen again but God sensed my hesitation. He rode upon my shoulders, pinched me, forced me to run clumsily through fields of rock, blew hotly into my ear, told me what I must eat and how long I must fast, forbade me to reply to the innocent questions of people I met, forbade me to accept their offerings of food or a bed, made my hair grow long and coarse, confused me with signs along the road because I could not read.

Why do you torment me? I cried out to Him.

But He remained close to me, hunched inside me and waiting for danger. Once, at the edge of a crowd, I caught a glimpse of a young priest and I saw in his face a brightness that was like my own, and I would have approached him to bless him except God restrained me at once, whispering: *He does not love you.* Another time He directed me to hide from some soldiers who were searching for me.

As I matured, my comeliness became a burden to me. I did not want to attract attention. I walked crookedly, with my body hunched over so that it should not attract the attention of women. I let my hair grow out wild and coarse and unwashed. Yet evil people sought me out. The pious knelt before me for my blessing and dared look at me only through their fingers; but the evil stared fully and curiously upon me and lusted after me. God whispered in my own hoarse shocked voice: *They are playing a game with your body in their heads. . . .* I wandered into the city of Lisbon and lived for a while in the Alfama, and wandered along the river, and though I wore only the shabbiest of clothes I was still sought out by the worldly, who seemed to recognize me more readily even than the pious.

I turned from them in shame but I could not escape them.

My manhood and my Godhood weighed heavily upon me. The eyes of the world were a vexation to me. Unescorted women, some of them foreign visitors, approached me to ask questions. I blessed them and they laughed in excitement; but they would not retreat, and laughed when I hurried from them.

One day an old man driven in a large black automobile signaled for his driver to stop, and while the old man gaped and leered at me the driver tried to talk me into getting into the car. *He is only an old man!—harmless!—wants to treat you to a ride—never been in a car, have you? Eh?*

The car was an amazing machine. I stared at it in fear.

Come, come with him, let him treat you!— you'll love riding in a car!

I found myself staring at the old man and

it occurred to me that he was in need of me, more desperately than the pious.

I accepted the invitation. The driver opened the back door of the great automobile with a bow, and I stepped inside. The interior of the automobile was so rich that my shabbiness was humiliating, but the old man did not seem to notice. He began at once to babble at me as if he were speaking to a child. His voice was sly and coarse: *I am sick—I require a blessing—I know you are a holy man—I've heard of you and I want you, only you!—but you are such a young man, hardly more than a boy?—you are loved by everyone, are you?—loved? how are you loved?— do you understand your own holiness, or is it fearful to you?—or is it a game?—do you accept money for your miracles?—will you perform a miracle upon me, eh?—do you love me as you love the poor?—do you love me in my sickness and age as you would love a fresh young girl?*

I told him that his sickness was an impurity of the heart.

He laughed. *Yes—of the heart—of the blood— an infection of the blood—my blood is in a fever and needs to be released!*

Now we were far outside the city; the driver had pulled over to the side of the road; he got out of the car and walked toward a forest and left us entirely alone; the old man, panting, clutched at me, his face brought up very close to mine and his eyes like hard knobs of glass staring into mine; he began to entreat me to save him, to cure him, to love him, to release him from his bondage, and God did not need to speak to give me instructions: I took out of my clothes a knife I kept wrapped in a rag and I pronounced my blessing upon the old man, sawing the edge of the blade across his sinewy throat until the skin burst, and, with my left arm crooked behind his head, I sawed at the tough flesh and bones until the head fell limply back and the evil rushed out of it in great spurts.

Now you are free, you are delivered of evil, I told him.

But after that my divinity was a torment to those I met. They were drawn to me, hearing of my arrival, and yet they did not dare approach me; just to glimpse me, hunched over as I was, my clothes in rags, was a shock to them; young girls wept and cried out in fear; men, who wanted to come to me as to a friend or a brother, were paralyzed and could not move; old women shielded their faces and trembled with terror.

God always instructed: *Go nearer, touch them, bless them!* But I did not want to sear their foreheads with my touch and I did not want to entwine myself in their nightmares.

I will drive these people mad, I thought.

My blessings were pronounced from hilltops, or at the edge of fields; one summer day, in a field of dying grain, I blessed an entire village and promised them a fine harvest, and suddenly their wretchedness struck me and I began to weep for them. I could not stop. As I wept, the sky gathered itself into great angry clouds; God told me to calm myself or there would be a storm; but the faces of the villagers caught at my eyes and I could not calm myself, my weeping increased, I began to sob like a child, and at once the sky gathered itself into storm clouds and rain began to fall, at first in hissing splotches, then in torrents, vicious and brutal as hail, striking down the fields of grain.

I ran from them and my running caused wind to be sucked after me—whirlpools of air struck out at the countryside and devastated it up and down the coast for hundreds of miles.

Where I wept, where I passed, there were floods and tornadoes.

I hid myself in the mountains, ashamed and terrified.

God prodded me to return to the people, but I had no heart for it; my Godliness was a torture to myself and to these people; I began to feel that I must put an end to myself. But first

I must see my mother once more. Though I was exhausted, I began the long journey home.

God battled and bucked inside me, and my face grew hot with His insults. *You are no Son of mine, but the Devil,* He cried. My mother must have got word of my coming, because she met me alone, at the outskirts of the village. She covered her face and led me back to our house.

For many days I lay in the dark. I prayed to God to forgive me, to allow me release and death, and in His spite He sent more torments upon me, for if I turned my head too sharply to one side—startled by a rat, perhaps—sudden storms would rush out in that direction, a hundred miles out into the countryside; if I turned my head too sharply to the other side, identical storms would rush out to sea. My hair grew longer. I could not cut it or wash it for fear of what this would do to the village—or to other villages, for this village was now leveled. All the people had fled. The castle was broken, its centuries-old walls fallen. Everyone had fled from me except my mother. But I did not dare to weep for them. I did not even dare scratch at the lice that infested my body.

You will leave this place, God commanded me; but I could not obey.

In the spring I walked out into the sunlight.

God's voice was a din in my head. My own voice wrestled with His, but feebly. I tried to instruct my mother but God interrupted me. I had great difficulty making her understand what my wishes were. She was an aged woman now, her eyes stark in her shrunken face, and it was the most sorrowful burden of my Godliness to look upon her and to see what I had done to her.

I was finally able to make her understand.

A tree behind our house served us. I rolled a boulder up to it—though God told me excitedly what this boulder was doing to our seacoast—and I stood upon it and extended my arms to fit along the symmetrical branches of the tree. My mother, grunting, climbed up close to me to drive the nails into my palms. I instructed her to avoid my eyes. The earth began to shake with the ferocity of my pain, but I did not cry out, and God gifted me with a spiteful vision of an entire town lost, the earth opening to receive it, its inhabitants crushed, but I did not flinch. Finally the nails were driven in, one thick nail in my left palm, two nails in my right palm, and I instructed my mother to roll away the boulder.

Now we are waiting for my death. I hang on the tree and am trying to die, but as the Son of God I am unable to cure myself as I have cured so many. I am unable to purify myself. God shrieks at me: *Always this happens! Always my sons disobey me!* I hang against the springy mimosa tree and wait with great patience for the fulfillment of my life.

The Murderer

✣

I was hurrying home, hurrying up the hill to my home, my legs straining with the effort, and on my right hand the cobbled street was deserted, still damp from a late afternoon shower, and on my left a high rough stone wall ran for an entire block. Some straggly, insect-eaten vines clung to the wall, but dryly, as if they might fall away at the slightest touch; they did not look living.

It was 5:25. The sky was still opaque with rain clouds, it was a fairly cool May afternoon, a Tuesday, my thoughts were busy with memories of the work I had left behind and expectations of the evening ahead, my wife's cheerful greeting and the odors of cooking that would pervade the house—and I glanced up to see someone hurrying toward me.

As I came up the hill, breathing quickly, this young man was coming down the hill. He was walking fast, unnaturally fast, as if he had to fight the impulse to break into a run. His eyes flew to my face as he approached me: he was of a squat figure, with an ordinary dark suit and a tieless shirt, his skin was sallow, even swarthy, but his eyes were oddly moist and bright, and I remember thinking that he was probably an intelligent young man—the brightest child in a family of peasants, their hope and their pride—

Seen from a distance, we must have been two similar figures moving rapidly together, one hurrying up a paved walk and the other hurrying down. We nearly brushed sleeves. I looked quite openly and genially at his face, wondering if I might know him—his hair was damp, and a small, thin cluster of curls had fallen onto his forehead—but he stared rudely at me and rushed by in silence.

I came to our gate, a doorway in the stone wall, but the gate was latched. It was no trouble to open it—the latch did not lock—but it was never kept latched and I remember thinking how odd this was. . . . Ascending the flagstone steps to our house I knew that something was wrong: the air seemed dislodged, as if someone had rushed through it. It was still quivering.

Inside the house I called out my wife's name in a sudden bright, shrill voice.

No reply.

I walked slowly down the dark corridor. No one in the drawing room—no one in the dining room— Ah, there, in the kitchen doorway!—a body lay crumpled in the doorway—

Vera, our maid.

I rushed from her and upstairs and there in our bedroom, there on the bed lay my wife herself—a small, crumpled body, a face turned up to the ceiling of the room, her pale clothes cruelly torn, yanked open, a bright flow of blood soaking into the bedclothes—

I fell toward the bed, screaming, losing consciousness—

When I was revived, I found myself lying in another bed, in another bedroom of the house. Maria, another of our maids, was weeping hysterically. The police were in the room, waiting. The doctor was leaning over me.

When I was able to talk, the police questioned me gently. I told them that I had come home from work as usual, I had discovered Vera's body downstairs, I had run upstairs to discover my wife's body—

"Did you see anyone near the house? Or out on the street?"

I stared at them.

"Did you encounter anyone at all?" the police asked.

"Yes. . . . I think so, yes. I think . . . a man. . . ."

"A man?"

"I think it was a man, yes. . . ."

"What did he look like?"

"Look like . . . ?"

His face was gone from my memory; his fleeing body, his fast-stepping legs, his bold dark stare. All gone.

"How old was he?"

"I don't know."

"A young man, a middle-aged man . . . ?"

I stared from face to face, as if these stern, patient faces might help me remember.

"I don't know," I whispered.

"You can't tell us how he was dressed, how tall he was, what class he appeared to belong to . . . ?"

"I don't remember. . . ."

And yet I must remember his face! must remember!

But the murderer's face had fled. Had faded. Was a blank: even his sallow ruddy skin had faded to nothing. His white shirt had billowed out in my mind's eye and blinded me, I could no longer see anything of his face or his body, I was blinded. . . .

The police questioned me for some time. They released me and I went to stay with my parents in Sintra.

I must remember his face! must remember!

My parents, who love me, wept and wrung their hands and tried to comfort me. They told me I must stay with them until the doctor said I was entirely well.

September came. Then winter, then another spring. Every afternoon I sit here in the garden, trying to remember the murderer's face. I am certain I will remember it soon. Sometimes the face is almost clear to me—I seize the dark eyes with my own once more, I see quite clearly the black curls, the rudeness of the mouth—and then it vanishes as if sucked into a hole, sucked back into nothing—

Yes. Nothing.

Impotence

At their first meeting she appeared slight and negligible in the body, a sixteen-year-old child with a sweet, forgettable face. He made a decision concerning her, and they were married. From above, he surveyed her: the frightened pale flesh of her body, the delicate features of a face he now owned. He made a statement to this small, tidy creature: "I love you."

After months of marriage, when he lay beside her in the dark he began to feel her as an equal; her weight balanced effortlessly against his, the bed equally divided. She was still a shy, inarticulate bride. But when he embraced her he felt with excitement and dread the slight tug of her flesh away from him, as if merging with the gravity of the room. She seemed more at home here, in this room, than he did though he had lived here for most of his life.

A year passed. At night he pressed against her, sometimes shivering, grateful for her body's warmth; her body gave off a sweet, generous warmth. He slept with his arm lying across her loosely. Sometimes he woke and felt, in the absolute dark, the warmth of the sun still in the swells of her body, held magically in her pores, like memory. In himself, warmth faded as soon as the day ended.

Her shoulders reared from him. Her chin was directed upward, as if she were staring into the next day, which he couldn't see. Her breasts had grown enormous, her stomach and abdomen like immense hills across which he slid, helpless. He memorized her flesh and observed in terror how the inches swelled. After the second year he could no longer get his arms around her; her legs, soft, unmuscular, grown thick as barrels, made his legs seem like a boy's.

Sometimes he fastened his lips to some part of her—the rounded flesh of a breast, the sturdy flesh of the upper part of her arm—but she was too large for him, too smooth, too swollen. He felt himself slide down helplessly from her. What if she turned upon him in her sleep? Could her flesh suffocate him? His entire body, lean and proud and highly trained, was no longer equal to the cavernous space between her legs.

As time passed he could lie safely only in the crook of her shoulder and neck, because he feared the sudden weight of her gigantic thighs and hips. He feared even her great soft torso. Her breath, which perhaps should have frightened him, had a hypnotic effect upon him: a delicate film of moisture formed almost imperceptibly over his face, masking him like gauze. He could breathe through this film, but with difficulty.

His fingers opened upon the swell of her cheek as if upon a sacred wall.

Letters to Fernandes
from a
Young American Poet

❦

Oct. 27

Fernandes:

Why are you running away from me?

Why do you fear me?

In your black Mercedes you drive one hundred miles an hour to get where I can't call out to you—you kneel anonymously in village shrines, in tiny chapels, you kneel and press your hands into your face, whispering to God. I know. I whisper to God also. Sick from eating clams last night,

I whispered to God also but God did not bother to listen. . . .

As far away as Oporto you've driven. Why do you fear me?

Your friend António is still missing. No official word yet where they are keeping him—hospital or jail. If the doctors say that António is suffering from "impaired judgment," people tell me, then he is suffering from "impaired judgment" and must be hospitalized. But which hospital? Where?

I walked around your family town house yesterday, circling it. Empty except for servants, who avoid me, fearful of my desperate Ohio accent. The police were not so fearful, only polite. Pretend a polite astonishment that I can speak and understand their language. . . .

Now it is morning and I wake up to António, the image of him in my head, and you, the image of you when you walked out of the café while I shouted your name after you—all of it like the taste of vomit. A film of vomit in my mouth.

Help him, Fernandes.

Oct. 28

Fernandes:
Up most of the night drinking and reading.

Read Whitman: "Agonies are one of my changes of garments." And: "Unscrew the locks from the doors! Unscrew the doors from their jambs!"

Do you know what he means?

Oh command me, give me a rifle, or money, give me a whispered message and I will obey you. You are twenty-five years older than I am and tired, yes, I know, the surprise of your friend's imprisonment is too much for you, I know, you liar and murderer. Can you hide from me? I will be brought to you, Fernandes, in one of your country houses, in a big laundry basket carried on the sturdy head and shoulders of a woman, Fernandes; try to hide from me!

People glance at me in the street. My untidy clothes and wild hair and tears. . . . Why is everyone in mourning here? Black clothes? Sunday clothes that wore out and are now worn during the week . . . ? They stare at me with gentle pity. I am not real to them. At the café I go from table to table with my petition, disturbing the dignity of the place, whispering, gesturing, a tall ungainly man who has no manners. The Portuguese could teach me manners. I never learned any in Youngstown or in New York. Did you ever get that far west, Fernandes, to Youngstown, Ohio? The suburbs grow in layers around the city, the air stinks, the houses are two years old and already grimy, while over here the houses are six hundred years old, the villages are a thousand years old, time is a pool here and your people glide silently through it, beautiful deathly people, sleepwalkers. Their eyes never quite come into focus when I talk to them. A River of Forgetfulness runs through the country. I keep stumbling into it, I will sink into it and die. . . .

I am drinking too much, my wife would say. She is a blond, thin, agitated woman I must have loved at one time. She has stopped writing. Today I picked up a letter at American Express, a friend at Stanford who wants to teach *The Sheathed Son of God,* where could he get hold of a copy? Couldn't find one in a bookstore even though António is "famous!" I won't bother to write and tell him that a few tattered copies of the book survive, Cuzco's translation, 1951, and my own of 1965, no point to it; my blood was drained into that book but it's out of print, what the hell, that life is gone and now we must think only of António, living. . . .

Read this letter. Read. Read what I am writing.

I walked around all day, up to the hilltop districts, wondering why the lines are broken. The connections are all broken. On the ground . . . I can almost see electric wires I must hop over, they're deadly, the sparkle is deadly and would kill me. . . . My wife's voice in my head:

please explain to me. . . . But I can't explain.
António's anarchy and love, António's simplicity.
. . . Can't explain. Can't explain why we must
come to grips with António's vision, why cross
& recross that Dark River of his when it is so
painful. Bringing the much-folded, much-un-
folded, much-folded petition to Pedra de Myra,
too old, blind. Bringing it around to the five or
six young poets you introduced me to—their bold
signatures—"bold"—as if they know they will not
be blamed. They are of good families, like you.

. . . trying to understand you and your
people, Fernandes. You are all sleepwalkers. Can
you explain yourself to me?

All A's books, all the *Legends,* are banned
here. You have lived with this for years. Will
you never do anything about it? When the language is erased we will all be erased. Pray, sink
your fingers into your eyes, you beloved of Our
Lady of Stone and of Dr. S, who had done "so
much a foreigner can't understand. . . ." We
will all be erased, all of us. I wrote to you that
the Price Foundation has dropped me, but you
did not reply. They said it had nothing to do
w/State Department interference or complaints
from officials here (never in their history had any
pressure been put on them, etc., anything "politi-
cal," etc.) in spite of A's ancient Communist ties.
A's "ancient Communist ties"—as if they hadn't

all rejected him, his gentle wise nihilism, twenty years ago! We are all being erased. There are magicians trying to convince us we don't exist, they are erasing us while we walk out in the sun or sink on our knees in remote limestone churches. . . .

Think of the humanity of the *Sheathed Son,* the beauty of those pages . . . can you abandon A? Can you forget him?

Oct. 28 11 P.M.

Fernandes:

It was an Italian magazine, name forgotten, that put me onto A's poetry. I read it all night long. Read it in a fever, in excitement, felt it— A's lovely language—like a wave that carried me with it, out of myself. It has carried me out of myself for years. Back home I discovered that a few people knew his name. I learned Portuguese just for him, to do honor to him, and to bring him into English more brittle, more precise, than Cuzco's (though I admire Cuzco's work). A's vision: love in all its Shapes, serpentine and ponderous Shapes, the denial of nothing, no landscape too ugly for him. I was born in Youngstown, Ohio, a city you have never seen, and it took me thirty years to get the smell of it from me. . . . How could I explain Youngstown to you? How could I explain any of us to you?

Iron, steel, barges, smokestacks, factories w/parking lots, acres of workers' cars—expensive shining new cars!—viaducts, railroad tracks, signal lights, glowing golden smoke, shopping plazas, kids w/jalopies, weighed down and heavy-heeled, we are in the very center of the world, where gravity is ten times what it is elsewhere, yet it's all precarious & brand new and could be blown away by the winds of your mountains. . . . You have had so many kings! Kings & killers & generals & saints & miracles. Nothing mean or small. Your imaginations are the size of the universe, but the universe is not well-lit. Our imaginations are the size of a high school gym, the bleachers pulled out for a basketball game, all lit up and noisy w/excitement, fun, kids bouncing the ball around, cheerleaders w/megaphones, girls on the bleachers w/their knees pressed together, watching the game, a closed universe, a closed Ohio universe, so different from yours. How did I get from that basketball court (I was damned good at it—six foot three, Fernandes, taller even than you!— and I was proud of myself, and still am, for that sad silly preposterous part of my life) to the eternal wind and the crash of the waves and the whitewashed churches and the medieval faces of your people, to A's passion & suffering & silence,

to this room where I am writing out my misery
& love to you, a stranger, because there is no one
else left . . . ?

Yes, I am proud of myself. I am proud of
having worked my way through the North American consciousness-slop, where so many young
poets, some of them older than myself, are perma-
nently stuck. How many of us broke through? I
think of Snyder & Kinnell & Bly. . . . Oh I
wanted to sit face to face w/A and explain my
love for him. I wanted to come out of myself
and "unscrew the doors from their jambs!" etc.
But over here it's like the inside of a vault, Edgar
Allan Poe, I am creeping & groping my way &
there is no explanation. . . .

No trial? No hearing? Not even a story in
the newspapers?

Looking down the dipping street to where
the boats are moored. Dizzy. Took eight rides on
the ferry. Rubbing my head against a railing
while a few tourists gaped. Sick at heart. Sick.
Don't even know where they are keeping him.
Sick from the sight of fish, big dead fish in
baskets, sick of the shells, the curving dipping
streets. Come all the way from Youngstown and
the hopeless raw ego of New York to where I
could weep for a man, really weep (have patience
with me—I can see your frown and your nervous
censuring scholarly scowl, Fernandes) and now

this, the blank faces, the walls, the police, the knowledge that for you people the Atlantic is the Substance of Life, and not the other direction, not people, not the human land that is real. Oh the Ocean is real & deathly. The Spirit that rises from it is deathly. That is why you seem so warm in your smiles & words and are so cold, transparent, forgetful in your shoulder shrugs and the insides of your heads & hearts.

Oct. 29

There is a solitary stone
A solitary perfect woman
Out of my side she bursts. . . .

When my translation of *Sheathed Son* came out, many people recognized A's genius and paid homage to it. They called him a "genius." Sales were good for a while, then in spite of Barker's long essay in the *Atlantic Review* it was allowed to die, the book went out of print, died, the "genius" faded & people were smug & silent. They yell "genius" all the time. I think the big prizes are awarded like this: the honored genius is lifted up on everyone's shoulders & paraded & thrown off the cliff, then everyone goes home satisfied; no, wait, they throw a monument over the cliff too, down on top of the man, to make sure he's dead & they are safe from him.

I am shouting at you. I am charged with making you understand: A must be freed, will be freed, if I have to die over here. If A and I both have to die. I have talked for hours, for days, w/people here who should understand, tried to project my idea (basically A's) of how the country could be transformed, nothing blown up or thrown into the air & raining down but a Spiritual change so much more violent—how all the countries of the world could be transformed, even the United States—what A saw, what he tried to make us see in his *Legends*.

. . . Must push ourselves out to the very edge of the Spirit.

. . . Must learn what A means by being "the beginning people."

Fernandes, meet me tomorrow! By the pool, the Praça de São Pedro de Alcántara! No one will know. Who was A for you, who was A in your heart & imagination?—bring him along w/you!

Oct. 30

Fernandes:

I waited for you all day. Steep hills, beautiful tree-shaded walks, beautiful black-clothed people, but no Fernandes. Or did I see you at a distance? The benign melancholy of your clothes, your expensive clothes, the slight stoop of your shoulders, the hesitant way you paused down the street, staring toward me—was that you, Fernandes, or another guilty bastard?

O came to tell me my days here are numbered—I gave him a shove—regretted it a minute later, he's so stupid & frantic himself. No police spy, they wouldn't have someone like that.

Waited all day.

Do you know if he is still living? Still "in good health"? There are so many whispers, rumors—talk of special treatments for dissenters in the "hospitals"—men who disappear—men without gravestones—yet the refrain is always, always: "What would we do without Dr. S?" "Who would die for us, except S?"

I puzzle over your kinship w/A, what his thirty years of visionary work meant to you. Dedicated that heartbreaking "Apocalypse" to you—to "Fernandes"— Read it over again. Again. Trying to understand. *What are we all doing here? What is this place we inhabit?* I think I am being initiated into something, you're the priest, the muttering mumbling black-gowned priest of the charnel house. . . .

Walked back toward the waterfront, alone. Masts of boats floating in the sunset. I felt the

back of my head crawl. I knew I wasn't on earth
but on Mars. This is Mars. Mars. Not earth, not
even the placid ocean-illuminated moon, where
I think I could survive. Here it is Mars and the
secrets are all in another language, the beatings
& torture are rituals behind walls, behind forgetfulness. The men I talk to, the men I scream at,
listen to my words and agree shamefully, helplessly, yet they forget as soon as they escape, the
way they will forget A. The River of Forgetfulness runs through all of you. . . .

In my suitcase I dug out that photograph
of you & A, taken in Paris 1951. Otherwise I
couldn't believe that A really exists/existed. A is
mustached, small, dark w/a bandit-smile & a small
beak of a nose—I could love him, could embrace
him so that his death & mine would disappear
in all the sweet fullness of our bodies—but he
eludes me, they have taken him away. You: the
"devout" Fernandes on the edge of A's life, taller
by half a head than A, strong in the chest and
shoulders, thick dark hair, eyegasses, the look
of a professor & a ruined patrician, long noble
nose, ascetic lips, etc. A owned nothing, not even
his books. They are gone. His mother has gone
to the north to live, "pensioned"—I couldn't see
her but I know what refrain she'd sing—*How
could we live, except for S?* She is "just a peasant,"
people tell me. Don't bother her. A owned noth-

ing, nothing was his in the end, not even his own books. The Apocalypse grabbed him up. The Earthquake came again and grabbed him up. He doesn't even own himself, his own language. What do you own? Half a dozen big houses—thousands of acres of land in Sintra—a palace? All in your famous family. But A has no family left. What is a family? I want to understand you but I can't because I don't speak Martian & what I translate into my head is not right. I don't understand what a family is. I gave all that up. Even my wife, that squalid selfish demanding creature that forbade me the embrace of other bodies, or A's body (as tender as his soul?)—I can't understand you because you all speak Martian, only my beloved A speaks to my soul, and they are killing him.

Oct. 31 6 A.M.

Fernandes:

In my own life I made bad hunches, bad guesses, but my blood has gone into my translations of A & I will stand or fall by the work I've done on him. I am satisfied. I am he and he is myself. Let the world sit in judgment on how his Flesh is Resurrected in my Midwestern soul. Poets & translators. Poets & lovers. Men & language. Men & men. Language.

I am imprisoned w/him, wherever he is. I share it. I am haunted by that face of his that I have seen only in photographs—is it such a Roman Catholic face as it appears? I would die for him, my life for his freedom. They want to throw me off the edge of the Martian cliffs into the ocean. . . .

The police strut by disguised as peasants.

I know you have left Lisbon. Don't dare to leave the country because that would look bad, but you've left Lisbon & are hiding somewhere. You have your own chapels, eh? And your own private priests? Is that how you people worship, on your humble obedient knees in front of the Virgin & her dreamy deathliness? But I could love her, yes—even her!—if A loved her—I could embrace her in all her stone, even her, even you!— if A showed me the way. Hatred for the Catholic-fascist-racist-colonizing-Martianizing culture—that was A's curse—but love for the faces, the beautiful faces, the Suffering we must endure in our loneliness—that was his sweetest burden, a curse too, because he couldn't escape.

A teaches us not to fear the Martian plains & oceans.

A teaches us not to fear the Shape-Changers —the evil magicians, black sorcerers of our dreams —as Blake saw also—but still in this cold room I am fearful of the changes that wait for me everywhere in this city—how I can't reach A & will never speak to him, how you have betrayed A in the shape of Judas, how I fear for you hanging yourself in the shape of Judas. . . .

Oct. 31   Noon

Fernandes:
I could have loved you too.

The Letter

❦

He stirs. His face threatens to swell with pouting.

"Why do you want it?" he asks.

"I want to read it again."

A nervous irritated movement of his head. "Why? You are tormenting me."

His hands moved together, to push me away. Pushing the air flatly away.

Timidly I explain, leaning forward: "I only want to read my letter again. Nothing more."

He stares out the window and down into the street. Why?

He has lost the letter.

Has thrown it away: crumpled it, ripped it

into pieces. Behind this pouting face I can see his face laughing at me.

"No," he says.

Magic. There is magic in his careless hands. We stare at them: all of us would stare at them if we could get close enough. We would kneel to be touched by them. He has broad blunt American hands. They belong on the steering wheels of American cars, the knuckles firm and white.

Suddenly I want to scream at him: *What did you do with my letter?*

Outside there is the perpetual noise—cars and trams. It is the background to his silence. The background to his sleep, when he sleeps in that bed during the day. The bed is always messy. Sleeping, his almond-shaped eyes are pure as a child's; the eyelids are like pure, sightless eyes that cannot stare boldly back.

We press forward to stare at his face.

The flesh has been so warmed by the sun, it is so humid and oily, that it seems about to swell and ripen like fruit. A full, happy face. Except now it is pouting.

He has dragged the cane-backed chair over to the window and he sits with his bare feet on the floor. His legs stretched out. Stubborn. He will not look at me. Near his feet there is a carton filled with a few greasy rags, leftover food. Flies crawl lazily on his bare feet. The skin twitches, and they rise again and settle again. He does not use his hands to brush the flies away. His hands gesture toward me, as if to brush me away.

"I was born of a humble family," he says, sneering. "But I won't be pushed around always."

The devils pricked me out of sleep this morning, very early. Tried to drive me here at once. But I was wise enough to wait. Now it is nearly noon and it is not strange that I am here. He will not think it is strange.

"I am not pushing you around," I tell him carefully.

He says nothing. I am sitting on a low stool— my large frame is bent over anxiously. Because he is turned away from me I may stare openly at him.

"Then you have lost the letter . . . ?" I whisper.

"No."

"Then you have thrown it away?"

"No."

"Have you given it to someone?"

"No."

It is June 12, 1968. I must go to the bank where there are telephone calls for me. But I am here in this house I have rented under the name of Fernandes. For thirty minutes I have been asking him to show me my letter to him, originally mailed last Tuesday to this address. But he stares out the window at the pavement of the street, which curves upward. It curves and turns indifferently, like the gesture of his hands.

My dear God, drive the devils from me. Then I will stand and wipe my face with my handkerchief and go out to my car and drive to the bank.

Perhaps he can read my thoughts, for now he looks toward me. He says: "It is here somewhere, look for yourself."

Ah. . . .

He seizes one bare foot in his hand and sits like that, smiling. Smiling at me with his mouth only.

He is from the South. From the seacoast and the region of earthquakes. He came here in April to live with his sister's family. I met him in a square, wandering like a tourist.

"I would be so grateful . . . yes . . . if I might look. . . . I only want to see again what I wrote. The words I wrote. I will leave the letter with you."

The smile does not fade.

He will bring the letter to my father: he will blackmail me.

When I get to the bank he will already be there. Waiting. With the letter in his hand.

He cannot read, of course. When the letter came to him here, the first letter he received, the only letter he has received, he waited for me in great excitement so that I could read it to him. Last Tuesday. Now he does not know where it is.

"Look for it. It is your privilege," he says.

I stand shakily. At once I want him to sink down again, to hide myself. He is staring so openly at me.

There are two things to do: find the letter and destroy it, or leave this place. The first way will be confused, shameful, as he watches me. The second would make him sorry for what he has done.

I cannot go away.

My father, who is seventy-eight years old, will die of shame instead. Then, when I imitate him, I will be imitating the speech and mannerisms of a dead man.

I go to the bed and stoop to look beneath it. Does he laugh softly? I look up at once, and then straighten again, though I have not really seen what is under the bed. Behind him the handsome Gothic window reaches up to the ceiling and dips back down again. He is from the South. So he has said and his accent bears him out. He is gone from here often. Perhaps he has not told me his correct name.

The bank is miles from this place.

"There was a fire down the street last night!" he says, just remembering it. He is boyish and something stirs warmly and cruelly in him.

There is another thing to do: to kill him.

I wander nervously around the room while he watches. This is a game. Is it a game? I hope it is a game and my letter is hidden from me, for me to discover.

Thin whistling breath of his: he forces air through his front teeth, which are uneven. There is a narrow gap between his two front teeth. If I glance back at him he will be smiling at me with that mocking smile and the air whistling between his teeth. One knee raised up to his jaw. One dirty ankle clasped firmly in his hand.

A bureau with two drawers, all untidy. Piles of towels, trousers, stained shirts. Such bright colors he chose. Why did he want such bright colors . . . ? If I dare to look back at him I will see that smile of his. Moisture comes into my eyes. I cannot see well. I hear birds outside the window, I see the shadow of a bird passing close in front of the window. I am afraid a bird will fly into the room and he will leap from his chair with a cry and catch it in his hands and bite off its head for a joke.

At home they did that, so he said. Not with pigeons but with smaller birds. He and his brothers. So he has said, but I am not certain that he tells the truth; when I doubt him I take off my glasses and rub the bridge of my nose with my thumb and index finger, wearily, and use this moment to close my eyes and hide from him.

No bird flies in the window.

In the square he was wandering, alone. Almond-shaped eyes. Very dark. A dark, rather low forehead. Black hair. A mouth sweet as oranges: the thought makes saliva run in my own mouth.

We ride in elevators often in other cities. Antiquated elevators. Like any boy—is he a boy?—he loves motion. He loves cars. Laughter escapes easily from him. But you must move fast to make him laugh, his head is so hollow that anything can fill it up.

Filth on the floor here. . . .

Can I send someone in to clean this? Do I dare send a woman in to see this?

The house is registered at the City Clerk's Office of Deeds under the name "Fernandes." It is a name I do not dare to carry around with me, fearing an automobile accident, an emergency, strangers sorting through my identification papers.

"Your life has no order," I say to him in a hiss.

"I don't hear . . . ?"

He has destroyed the symmetry of Lisbon for me. Now this half of the city, his half, draws me to it. The other half springs away, light and useless. Not wanting to weep in front of him, I take off my glasses and rub the sore bridge of my nose.

I return to the search. Papers in a corner. Candy wrappers of bright colors, like his shirts. Newspapers I have brought here. The gazette I read to him, the comic papers, to teach him to read; a joke; he falls off his chair like a boy, settling in his chair for a lesson and then falling off, pretending that he is so stupid.

I am afraid he will fall off his chair now and burst into laughter.

"Last night there was a fire. This morning I walked to the waterfront," he says shrilly. "I have a lot of thinking to do."

I am bent over and my face is red to bursting.

"Yes, I have thinking to do. I am of a humble family but people can't push me around. I will not be pushed around."

He wants me to look at him but I will not turn.

Many weeks ago, in April, he was wandering and his eyes wandered onto me. I saw he was a boy, fifteen or sixteen years old. Later I saw he was a boy nineteen, maybe twenty years old. His chest is short and full, the hairs sparse, black, and coarse like the hair of his head, to drive me crazy. The surfaces of his body undulate like the streets of our city.

The Letter

This debris is his life. It is his life here. He throws his things into a pile, he lives in a heap, it is all that he knows. He will be fat and ugly in ten years and no one will love him. But it is June 12, 1968, and my eyes are stinging and I am not able to run away.

". . . you want to take away the key?" he says boldly.

Now I think: *I have won. I am stronger than he is.*

"You want the key back? Take it. Take it back."

Singsong words.

Dear God, help me to find the letter. . . .

More comic papers. Splattered with something foul that has dried. Why does he save them? Will he take them back home to read to his younger brothers? To move his finger beneath the words and pretend to read?

And then I find it—the letter.

But it is not my letter.

I straighten up. My knees and thighs ache. I am not well. The letter is on stationery from one of the hotels and it says:

You are from the land of earthquakes
Glass shatters in your mouth
I give you this white powder of such
    sweetness

You will never guess that it is really glass.

The handwriting is arrogant, in dark green ink. The spelling is perfect.

I stand transfixed as I read this message. My eyes beat with blood and I feel myself passing into this piece of paper, the stiff paper, I feel myself shouting these words at him and knowing I will receive no answer. He is not very interested, really. He is looking at my car down in the street. He is thinking about a ride, but a ride is out of the question until night. So he is not even thinking about a ride or the car or me.

I am this other person. Behind the words: I am behind the words. I am writing these strange words to him, hiding my nervousness behind the stiff sloping letters. I am pretending to be an American, maybe, with another continent over my shoulder. I am not thinking of his eyes and mouth or his dirty ankle clasped in his hand, I am not thinking of the reddened insect bites on his thighs that he scratches to bleeding, I am not thinking of his face wild and distorted during our first argument, and his tears.

"Ah, did you find it?" he cries.

He is very relieved. Gets to his feet.

Yes.

"Yes."

"You found it . . . ? Good!"

The Letter

He stands beside me and squints at the letter, nudging me. He does not know he is nudging me.

"Good," he says. "Now you are happy?"

"Now I am happy."

I must leave. I must fold the letter carefully and put it in my pocket. But if I am killed in an accident they will take it out of my pocket and unfold it again. . . . I put it in my pocket while he watches. I draw my hands over my eyes. I am not well. The passion of this message beats in me, in my very fingertips. It joins with my own.

I cannot make any choice. One letter, another letter—one man, another man—what does it matter? What does it matter which of the two men I am?

The sweetness of the noon washes over me and I give myself up to it without question.

Plagiarized Material

Loving words. Loving. Enduring odors of people, blurred faces of people, not the true syntax of nouns and verbs and parts, joints, nerves, networks, page-miracles finer than the stars, all small enough to love, miniature as the shrewd iris of the eye. . . . He loved words. He loved. They were the correct size for his love. Magnified, they would have terrified him.

But:

Comfortably monastic, the proper life of Cabral and his quiet earned fame. Not fame, not "famous," a vulgar word, but the created miniature fame of the author of the following titles: *Metaphors, A Body of Words, In the Mind of the Brain of C, Lex, Semblance and Substance,* all intricate works defining themselves as works, words on pages, the printed words actual works of art, printed on pages, their shapes and unique destinies only there on the page, an absolute creation. When Cabral was younger, in fact a prodigious child whose brain burned for books, whose meager health never prevented him from hours of exhausting research in the Museum of Ancient Art, he had written an extraordinary "meditative" study of the polyptych of the "Adoration of St. Vincent," not quite art history or art criticism or poetry, one hundred pages that had astonished some of his teachers and dismayed others, seemed to have no visible effect on his father at all, and convinced his mother that he was a genius. That was in 1939. The study was privately printed, with costly illustrations in full color, and Cabral, sixteen years old, held the book in his hand and turned it over and over, as if it were a sacred thing, in a way beyond his own possession. He loved it fiercely. He learned how to love.

The father died.

Cabral, obeying his father's instructions, had begun his study of law and, though he detested it—these volumes of words that *were not his own—*

he continued his studies and received his degree; in fact, his performance as a student of law was so praiseworthy, his teachers were so impressed, that Cabral wept when his mother told him: "Now that your father is dead. . . . Now you are not his." Cabral wept because it was true; because he need not obey his father, he need not go into law or "into" anything else; his father would not know how excellently he had/would have done. The mother, arthritic and peevish and very vain, told him that he must use his talent to honor the family, to glorify the family. Cabral, who was working late at night on a study of the influence of Oriental art on sixteenth-century ecclesiastical plate, a work composed in blank verse, stood at her bedside and hesitated only a moment before telling her he would obey.

"Take no more than two or three years," she said. Near the end of her life her voice was raspy, broken, and yet powerful. "I want to see the book. I want to hold it. Do you understand?"

He understood.

So he remained at home. His paternal great-grandfather had begun a tradition of government service, approached by way of the law, but Cabral, who had hated the law anyway, knew he did not have to continue that tradition. Of course there was no financial need, since the family's copper and tin mines in the north assured them a large income. Cabral was proud of his family, of the name itself, *Cabral,* because the very sound symbolized a rich, musical, almost magical power: anyone who heard it would be forced to think immediately of the explorer Pedro Alvares Cabral, claimed as an ancestor though exact historical proof was missing. It did not matter to the young man that this "ancestor" was questionable, or even that he had existed at all. The man himself, the sixteenth-century man, had no interest to Cabral in the twentieth century . . . why should he have any interest? . . . Cabral, the twentieth-century Cabral, honored only the word, *Cabral,* which seemed to him mysterious and holy.

Whether the explorer was an ancestor or not, the Cabrals had, for the past century or more, begun to emigrate to Brazil until, at about the time of the young man's father's death in 1949, the family that remained at home was known only as the "Lisbon branch." The New World had proved to be a stubborn weight, tilting the surface of the earth and unsettling things once believed to be fixed. But Cabral rejected it, as his father had. He did not reject it for his father's reasons, however—his father had "loved" this country—but because he had no interest in any world, New or Old, sensing himself superior to such material oddities.

Then Cabral's older brother was killed, at the age of twenty-nine, in an unaccountable motor accident on the highway to Estoril, and Cabral became the last male heir of the family; after the marriages of his sisters, he became his mother's last male companion, her last possession. He loved her, in a deferential and patient manner, closing his mind against her repetitive complaints about bad health, bad weather, ungrateful children and relatives, sordid private doings among the nation's "great men"—she had never forgiven Dr. Salazar for remaining neutral during the Second World War and for allowing certain nations the use of the Azores. He tried to love her, murmuring to himself the curious word *love*, while she continued her raspy embittered monologues. But, dissatisfied as she might appear, she always concluded her speeches by telling him how proud she was of him, of the way he had devoted himself to his exhaustive history of the Cabral family, "and saved yourself from going your own way," she said. She meant the way of the poet, perhaps. Cabral was not exactly sure.

She died when the history was only one-third completed, but he knew that she died secure in the knowledge he would finish it; which he did. By this time he was thirty-nine years old. The five-hundred-page book was privately printed, at an expense that startled even the usually placid

Cabral, but it was a beautiful creation—with twenty-five photographs in full color of the old places, some of which went back to the eleventh century, four of which had been graced with the visits of kings. The last photograph showed the house Cabral had inherited, the family town house in Lisbon: it was fairly new, having been built at the turn of the century, with several stories of open loggias, and a façade made heavy and turgid by a series of projecting piers, in the "plateresque" style. Its white limestone had weathered to a handsome golden brown. It was a striking house, near the upper end of the Parque Eduardo VII, with a view over the lower part of the city and the Tagus and the Bairro Alto hills. Inside, its ornamentation tended toward the almost fantastical, so that Cabral, conscious of a certain visionary absurdity in it, often apologized for it by saying: "This house has absorbed the gothic, the oriental, the modern—not a work of art but many works of art, jumbled together and therefore canceling one another out."

And to himself he would add: *Unlike me.*

Free now of the obligations of the past, he began a period he was to consider experimental, though the critics who, a dozen years later, began to assess his work, were to call it "traditional." He did a grave, seemingly pious, but slyly mocking monograph on the Cathedral of Santa Maria of Évora, which dated back to the turbulent medieval era and about which, over the centuries, many bizarre legends had attached themselves. Cabral's ingenious, almost ascetic wit in cataloguing these legends was lost on most of his readers, who were grateful for his unusual synthesis of "history" and "piety." Then, sensing himself so superior to his readers that he must instruct them in the knowledge of himself, Cabral the author, he wrote an entire novel—*The Legend of Salúquia*—in exactly the style and with exactly the heavy allegorical moralizing of Eça, whom he of course detested, and, of course, the novel was hailed as brilliant. *Accomplished with the power and the love of Eça himself,* the nation's most influential magazine intoned, *in fact, it may be suggested that Cabral is already Eça's master....*

Cabral waited several months, then sent a succinct statement of his aesthetics to the magazine's editors; this "aesthetics" explained, with a most formidable mocking clarity, how the "Eça" novel was a parody and how its author, Cabral, had set himself the task *as an artist* to master the form of the novel simply so that he might discard it. The essay was later expanded into Cabral's book of related essays, *In the Mind of the Brain of Cabral,* in which he made statements that had a far-reaching effect on young writers, primarily in France and in the United States, though also, rather unexpectedly, in Portugal itself. Small as Cabral's readership was, he became rather famous for these remarks:

> All my writing, as it is written, cancels out the tradition in which it is written. It is not magic, but anti-magic. It has no meaning. It *is*. It is not even "mine." As you read it, it is not "yours"—and, in fact, as you read it, "you" cease to exist. I work with words. The words *are* only themselves; they have no purpose outside themselves. They are hieroglyphics on a page but, unlike hieroglyphics and all crude symbols of man's futile quest for meaning, they hold no meaning; they "are" not even themselves. All my writing is destined to prove that "writing" (and reading) does not exist; "writers" (and readers) subsequently do not exist.
>
> The world releases a stench; the world is not equal to any subjective, specific, anti-magical assault upon it. That is why my

writing reduces the world to words
and, ultimately, words to silence.

An English critic, author of a work on
Wittgenstein, came to Lisbon to talk with Cabral,
anxious to meet the man who had made such
declarations and had, in support of them, written
such iconoclastic prose fictions; but Cabral refused
to see him. He was shy, yes, but stubborn as
well. He wanted to be the only "critic" of his
own work and, while he was flattered that so
prominent a man should want to see him, he
resented the fact that his aesthetics and his spare,
ingenious, self-annihilating prose must be inter-
preted by others and wrenched from him. Though
he was frigid in his dismissal of the critic, the
man later published a long, exclamatory, entirely
laudatory essay on Cabral, in both England and
the United States, claiming that Cabral's work
(including even the early "family history," which
was now eagerly bought and claimed as "anti-
history") was "revolutionary" fiction, that its
supreme beauty was its refusal to be a "digestion
of life" like most art, avant-garde as well as bour-
geois and traditional. . . ."Cabral," Cabral read,
in spite of himself seduced by his critic's generous
praise, "is at once Cabral and anti-Cabral, Self
and Anti-Self, as his art is both Art and Anti-Art.
Cabral refuses to order experience for us; he

190

scorns to 'give a meaning' to life; he scorns life itself, thereby freeing his readers from the centuries-old, tedious, boring sentimentality of the illusion of psychological reality. It is not simply that Cabral so beautifully refuses to lead us into a 'higher morality' (for innumerable modern writers have made this courageous refusal); he cancels out morality itself, he obliterates it by the cerebral perfection of *words*."

Reading this essay, Cabral began to feel a little dizzy. It was such high praise! He had known, or sensed, that he was a genius . . . yes, surely, a genius, but . . . but he had not exactly realized the extent of his genius. . . . He was dizzy with excitement, with an emotion he did not recognize. Half detesting himself for his boyish vanity, he read the essay through again, and then a third time . . . yes, a third time, feverishly skimming all the by-now familiar words ("revolutionary fiction". . ."scorns life itself". . . "cerebral perfection of *words*"). He had to admit, finally, that this brilliant English critic had understood him. This expert on Wittgenstein, according to a biographical note the author of several books on poetry and linguistics, in addition to the Wittgenstein study, this total stranger, had had the insight to comprehend Cabral's art. What a triumph for him! . . . as it was, in a way, a defeat for Cabral himself. He smiled ironically, thinking of *Cabral* passing into literary history, into a limited but powerful fame; *Cabral and Anti-Cabral*.

That night he woke from sleep, startled. He must have been dreaming.

But he could not remember any dream; he remembered only an idea, a pure stream of words, a warning: *They will appropriate you.* He sat up, switched on his bedside light, tried to calm himself. He had not experienced a dream, he had experienced only an idea. But it had come to him with the irrational, shameful power of an old-fashioned dream. *They will appropriate you.* He tried to distract himself by looking at the room around him—the antique furniture, the walls, the velvet drapes. This was real, this room. Wasn't it real? His heart began to pound strangely. It was real, of course; he had slept in this bed, with its carved bedposts, for decades. . . . The style of ornamentation did not exactly please him, for he had more classical tastes; nevertheless he changed nothing in the house, not even in his own bedroom. Most of the decorations were in the baroque manner, the heavily gilded wood of the door and the archway alive with twisted figures of angels, floral motifs, grapes and vines, birds, fruits. . . . They seemed almost to be moving, writhing, as he stared. Some had invaded the ceiling, enormous cherubim the size of human children. . . .

Cabral got out of bed. He hurried to his study in order to check something in the Englishman's essay.

He skimmed it again hurriedly. Yes, it was as he had thought. Yes. Some of these ideas, the very phrases and exact words, the *exact words*, were Cabral's. But they were part of a story he had begun months ago and temporarily set aside in order to work on a series of mock love sonnets. The story, untitled, had been a clever "story within a story within a story," centering on a writer much like Cabral, who was quite arrogant in stating the terms of his own aesthetics, the terms by which he demanded his fiction be judged. Cabral looked through his drawers, feverishly pawing at notes, papers, folders . . . almost, almost he wished the unfinished story would be missing, so that he might believe the Englishman had stolen it. *That* he could accept. Plagiarism he could accept. . . . He located the story, hardly a story at all, only an outline and a few scrawled paragraphs. It was strange, Cabral thought; why had he imagined this story was nearly completed? There was very little to it. But there, on the first page, in his own handwriting . . . there he read these words: ". . . the story is to be both myself and not-myself, Art and Anti-Art. What use the stink of morality? Obliterate it by the cerebral perfections of *words*."

He was quite frightened. He looked from the essay—published in a handsome, glossy-paged American magazine—to his meager notes and back again, struck by the closeness of ideas, phrasing, even words. The very words were similar! Cabral wondered if he were losing his mind. But . . . but. . . . He tried to regain his sense of humor: it was a coincidence. A bizarre, disturbing coincidence but, like all coincidences, in fact like everything, it was meaningless.

In the morning, when he returned to his study, he saw the essay with its pompous title, "Cabral and the Garden of Adonis," and his own tablet pages of notes, lying on the desk where he had dropped them. He seized them and ripped them into pieces, threw the pieces away, and forgot about the freakish experience.

In fact, he threw himself into work, a series of poems in a deliberately strained, mawkish idiom, "love" sonnets of a kind never written before. They represented a challenge to him, beyond simply the literary virtuosity demanded, for they required him to rake his memory, parts of his unvisited memory . . . some years ago he had been in love, he had been "in love," or in "love," he was not quite certain of the terminology that defined his experience. For several days he simply made notes in his rather crabbed, irregular handwriting on unlined sheets of in-expensive tablet paper; he always used this kind of paper because it reminded him of his child-hood, his school years, when he both was and was not Cabral. He tried to remember precisely what he had felt, though it was not "he" who had felt those emotions, but an earlier, lesser self. He believed he had been "in love" at the age of twenty, which would have been in 1943. But his memory was curiously blank. There must have been a recognizable human object for his love, but he could not quite remember her . . . "her" . . . though he knew that the girl had married someone else decades ago, and had drifted entirely out of Cabral's consciousness; which was quite natural. Perhaps she did not even live here in the city any longer. Perhaps she was dead, long dead. That did not matter at all, and yet it dis-turbed him that he could not force his mind to truly recall the emotions he had felt for "her." He remembered a long period of time, an amazing six or eight months, that had passed in a night-marish sequence of jerks and surges, in which he, the twenty-year-old Cabral, had not been in control of his emotions at all. Only the rigor of his studies and the nightly hours of writing in secret (from the hour of midnight until two o'clock, each night), had kept him whole and sane. The girl had been his own age, she had had a fair, pale complexion . . . dark hair . . . dark eyes . . . like everyone else. Cabral wondered if, given a premise, he might deduce her in a logical manner. The premise might be: *All Portuguese girls have these traits.* . . . No. *Most Portuguese girls have these traits.* . . . But the "most" invalidated the syllogism and Cabral lost interest in it. What a waste of his valuable time! He was beginning to feel restless. The task he had set before himself, quite deliberately, was formidable and heroic and, after the sonnets—the "metasonnets"—were published, perhaps in a few months, he would hint in a prose piece at their design, their function, the advance they represented in his art. In fact, he knew absolutely what he intended by these metasonnets and, though he was temporarily balked at writing them, he experienced no difficulty at all in writing of their interior meaning. He put down the tablet and went to his typing table, and typed without hesitation the following paragraph, to be included in his last book, *Semblance and Substance*:

> The "Pillory" sequence, which appeared to be in prose, was actually —as discerning critics may have noticed—made up of Petrarchan sonnets linked by a sound common

to each unit. The usual mechanical
and tedious division between the
octave and the sestet was rigor-
ously observed, in order to annihi-
late such devices not only for the
future (for no one writes such
mawkish sonnets today) but for
the past: after my "Pillory," no one
will read any Petrarchan sonnets
without laughing. The Shake-
spearean, or English, sonnet is of
course too crude in its structure
for my interest; it is its own
parody, and before such complete-
ness an artist like myself, in all
humility, must be silent.

This pleased Cabral immensely; he read it through
again and could not resist adding:

The task before me was complex:
which must take priority, the exorcising of an emotion, or the exorcising of an entire literary tradition? Beyond this, there is the quite
reasonable hope that the reader
who is sensitive enough to my art
will, himself, join me in exorcising
these outmoded aspects of intel-

lectual life. That is to say, he will
relearn, re-experience, regain the
uncontrollable emotional excesses
he suffered when (1) he loved (2)
he read any/all of the Petrarchan
sonnets. Then, reading "Pillory," he
will not only reject these excesses,
not only forget them, but *erase*
them—which is the magic of the
most sensitive art, annihilating
all private and public experience up to the moment at which
the writer/reader exists. Beyond
that. . . .

He stared dreamily out the window.

No, he must not put forth any more of his
aesthetic theory in this particular essay; he would
save it for another. So he X'd out the words
Beyond that . . . though with some regret.

He left the typewriter and took up the
tablet again, feeling refreshed. Now that his goal
was firmly stated, it should not be difficult for
him to create the work of art that embodied it;
almost, perhaps, the "work of art" would create
itself, or was irrelevant. *That* was a thought: the
work of art *was* irrelevant.

Cabral felt a peculiar dreaminess.

But no, he would save that insight for an

even later essay. Since the publication of *A Body of Words*, which had been enthusiastically reviewed nearly everywhere, including, now, to Cabral's surprise, rather unheard-of local newspapers in cities of America that had long seemed to him "names" of cities meant to be outrageously comic and not "cities" at all (how the range of one's delight in absurdities was always being expanded!), Cabral had received dozens of letters from magazine editors, begging him for contributions of any length; even paragraphs or parts of paragraphs. And so he had no reason to hurry, to rush his aesthetic theory into print. In fact, he rather liked the method forced upon him by the multiplicity of journals: he believed in fragments, essentially. He preferred fragments. Like those hideous blue and white *azulejos* found everywhere in the country, his work was basically in parts, not wholes, and must be put together by someone else, someone who believed in the trashy happiness of the *total picture*.

By now several hours had passed and he had failed to remember the "girl" at all. His mind moved steadily away from her; she was not a sufficient weight, a pinpoint of dense gravitation; she lacked any interest to him at all. . . . All he could remember was a drive with her nearly into Spain, so long and vexing a drive, during which . . . during which their "love" was discussed and . . . and there must have been hours of dialogue, there must have been . . . sufficient emotions behind the words to justify the experience. . . . He recalled quite vividly, however, stopping for a meal at Frexo-de-Espada-à-Cinta. This town was to be their farthest venture, though at the time neither Cabral nor the girl had known it; immediately afterward, Cabral headed back for home. Something had evidently been decided there. While the girl had been elsewhere—in a shop?—Cabral had found himself staring at the pillory in the village square. The Pillory. The pillory of 1943 would become *The Pillory* of Cabral. Metasonnets in prose form. It was a handsome enough pillory, the original cage hidden by a superstructure in the form of a prism. Cabral, the young man of twenty, had stared and stared at the pillory there . . . that day . . . a late afternoon sun, a kind of beauty, grace, holiness in the light . . . illuminating in all its medieval sturdiness the center of village life, this village or any village, or any town, any city, any "life" whatsoever. . . . His mind seized the image, the symbol, fastened upon it eagerly. How perfect a symbol for human existence! At the center of the square at the center of the village at the center of the country at the center of the world there was the *pillory*. Nothing else. The original cage in which miscreants were locked, the original

iron hooks to which they were chained, were
gone now, in this century and on this particular
day; no more public exposure or hangings or
torture. But. But the pillory itself did remain.
It *did* remain and Cabral thought himself justi-
fied in reading it as a symbol; he *would* read it
as a symbol. Almost, almost . . . but this was
fanciful . . . almost the young man of twenty
had known that the elder Cabral would, decades
later, be seeking the perfect image for a work
of art, and the vivid memory of that column and
its prism would flash into his mind. Of course,
even the crudest of academic critics would note
the relationship between the pillory and the May-
pole and the Tree of Life and the Cross and the
Tower of any authority and the Phallic Principle
and. . . .

Dreamily, he thought of the assessment his
admirers would be forced to make of the metasonnets. He was controlling them, really. He was
writing, through them, the theory of his art!

Finally he put his work aside and returned
to his typewriter.

That was on a Monday in one of the spring
months; that summer, at the family home in the
Sintra, Cabral opened a package of books he had
ordered from a French bookseller, and, idly leafing through a thin volume by a poet whose name
he had not heard before, he came across a poem

called "The Pillory." But it was a poem—no, it was not a poem, exactly—it was in the shape of a column, rather thick on the page, perhaps three inches of type. It looked, indeed, like a pillory. Cabral, startled, trying not to become too alarmed, skimmed through the prose-poetry and saw that it was *his*. It was *his*. Not in the Petrarchan form, but in this ugly visual form. . . . He felt that he was losing his mind. He got to his feet, upsetting the terrace table and the books, and stared in terror at the familiar garden—the graceful walks, the flowers, the glossy leaves of the cork oaks—all familiar, familiar—there should have been no terror here—

He was breathing oddly, not in rhythm with himself. Out of rhythm. Someone else was breathing for him. He felt the lungs filled, emptied. A terrible fist beating: his heart.

He must have stood there for some time. A servant appeared at the periphery of his vision, but with an abrupt gesture Cabral dismissed him. Then, growing calm again, he uprighted the table; he picked up the books, the package, even the thick twine. He would always be a fastidious man, he told himself ironically, even if he went mad.

So, with a regained sense of detachment, an almost literary detachment, he examined the book of poems. They were in French, but by a man named Kiewicz, said to be one of the most brilliant of the new generation of Polish poets. Kiewicz! Cabral had never heard of him. The title of the volume was *Approaching Silence*; the poems were all in shapes, shadowy shapes of things like pine cones, stars, spires, fists. How crude and unremarkable! Cabral felt a mist of pure rage pass over him. He read and reread "The Pillory" and noted, in spite of his anger, how cleverly the young poet had used all of his, Cabral's, insights in this recollection and dismissal of young love. Yes, it was all there; not Petrarchan, but still quite brilliant. Indeed, brilliant. Some of Cabral's own words ("why carve, why erect, why not shellac? why not new verbs of Plasticate?") seemed more effective here, on the thick expensive cream-tinted page, in this columnar shape, than they had in Cabral's own prose.

He laughed bitterly. Laughed. Someone laughed. He felt the constriction of lungs, stomach, throat; someone laughed in his place. At this very moment, upstairs in his desk, were the galleys for "The Pillory," scheduled for October publication in—what ugly coincidences!—a French literary journal. The prose-poem was to appear with a translation done by Cabral himself. But now he would have to inform the editors that . . . that "The Pillory" could not be printed . . . because . . . because . . .

No, he was losing his mind.

Yet he was not losing his mind: "The Pillory" was a poem evidently written by someone named Kiewicz. Cabral turned to the back of the book and read, to his shock, that Kiewicz had been born in 1951! "My God, he is so young . . ." Cabral whispered. There was no photograph of the mysterious Kiewicz. Only black print on a white, white strip of paper that announced solemnly that the young man had been educated at Warsaw and at the Sorbonne, that in 1967 an exhibition of his and his wife's paintings had caused "great controversy and excitement" in Paris, and that since that time Kiewicz was devoting himself to poetry that "evoked and annihilated physical shapes and physical displacements of air in the human universe."

Cabral threw the book aside.

"I am/am not losing my mind," he stated.

And so, after that time, during the lethargic summer months in the country and well into the autumn, Cabral worked only fitfully on a new work: a mock-mystical celebration of Our Lady of the Mountain Belvedere, an intricate prose-poem elaborately cross-referenced with earlier works of his own, so that the attentive reader or critic would hear echoes . . . echoes of Cabral

. . ."Cabral". . . . *As we experience this amazing work we re-experience Cabral himself, who, in himself, re-creates the history of consciousness for us and obliterates it . . . into a silent future.* . . . Someone would write that sentence, a man, somewhere, a man brilliant enough to understand the work. Perhaps an American, perhaps an Englishman, perhaps . . . perhaps, a Polish poet, writing so beautifully in French? Cabral had begun to age. He had not been born in 1951. "Unfair, unfair," he sighed. He sensed an army of young men, as sensitive and evil as Kiewicz, plagiarizing the works of Cabral before they were written.

The winter was especially gloomy and wet in town; Cabral sat for long sluggish hours at his window, seeing nothing. Sometimes he worked on the poem, sometimes he spent an entire morning leafing through new books, journals. He knew . . . he knew. . . . He *knew.* The poem had already been written. He knew. But, until he actually discovered it, until that terrifying moment, he supposed he must force himself to keep writing. . . . But, one day in December, he was rewarded for his diligence: he found "Our Lady of the Mountain Shasta" in an American journal, Cabral's work exactly, though in another setting and with names—"names"—names not familiar to him; evidently names of things that existed, or did not exist, or partly existed in California.

The journal was thick and handsome, its pages glossy, tinted green. Cabral did not bother to read about the poet who had "written" this poem, only to note that his name was not Polish (it was O'Wicca, a tri-syllable horror Cabral could not have invented himself) and that the essay facing the prose-poem was titled "The Epistemological Structure of Witchcraft."

Cabral's father had had an excellent wine cellar, well-stocked with a wine from the Lower Douro Valley, his favorite, a white wine sometimes appearing golden, very light and lightly bitter; though Cabral's father had been a quite content man, even a cheerful man, he had drunk this wine to "calm his soul," or so he said. Cabral himself had never cultivated much interest in wine, but now he began to drink, wondering if he might "calm his soul" in this way. But bitter, bitter was his soul, and the taste of his dead father's wine . . . so he began to drink a sweet red wine from the Dão Valley, sensing a futility even in this, even in lifting the crystal glass to his lips. . . . After a while the wine, far from seeming sweet, seemed bitter: a frantic concentration of sugar, so strong that it was actually bitter, like arsenic. Cabral wondered idly if arsenic and sugar looked alike.

If so . . . ?

Did that symbolize something? Or . . . ?

Or did it symbolize nothing?

Or did it symbolize a thought?

There was a single week in January during which Cabral discovered three future works of his, in quite separate journals, each with a title that resembled the titles in his notes (an untidy pile of papers scattered in his workroom), each with a clear, logical advancement of the work Cabral had outlined, and each . . . most horrible truth of all . . . each superior to the work Cabral himself would probably have written. He realized this, could not deny it. It was true. One Miltonic poem of thirty pages, called "Solar Hostility Vapors," by a young man/woman (Cabral could not judge by the name, which was simply "Caper") was, in its evocation of Milton's poems, *including his early Latin poems,* and . . . most astonishing of all . . . *including the critical assessments of his poems by Samuel Johnson* . . . a feat of anti-magic that Cabral, lacking a really comprehensive knowledge of English literary history, could never have written. He was able, but only barely, to appreciate it. He was able to sense that Milton and his critics and (perhaps?) everyone who had read them had been . . . or should have been . . . annihilated by this poem. . . . But. . . .

The Poisoned Kiss

How he despised his Plagiarist Masters! He knew they were much younger than he. They would outlive him. They bred shamelessly and multiplied, like the lowest forms of animal life . . . or plant life. . . . Cabral wished them all dead. But. But they would probably not die. Who would die? Did it matter? He was seized by a sudden inspiration: mockingly, hatefully, he would compose a quite banal, "sincere" little essay, and one of the Plagiarists would steal it and be subjected to scorn.

It was the first thing he had written in months, a single-page essay "On Humility," in which he forced himself to imitate the kind of intolerable, pompous essays he and his classmates had had to translate from Latin into Portuguese so many years ago. What empty rhetoric! What waste! It took him many hours to write it, but finally he finished it and felt an odd, bitter glow of satisfaction. The Plagiarist who dared steal this essay would be mocked by everyone. . . .

But on the following Sunday, in fact only three days later, Cabral glanced through a popular newspaper and there, in the multicolored feature section, there, there was "On Humility," written by a Lisbon "man of letters" who had been around for many years, who had published fifteen or more incredibly wretched, banal, "uplifting" novels about the holiness of the peasant,

the soil, the crude beautiful pleasures of life. . . .
This novelist, whose name was almost a joke
among intelligent, educated people, lived in an
elegant home in Estoril; he was a wealthy man
and had made his own fortune, raising himself
from a boyhood spent in a northern fishing village.
Cabral read the essay all the way through and
noted how, precisely, the novelist had followed
Cabral's sentences. The inflated, strained piety
. . . the overlong Latinate constructions . . . all,
all appropriated without the slightest altera-
tion. . . .

And so everything was lost.

And so, he thought bitterly, he had learned
humility.

When one of the maids entered his study
hours later, he stared at her in alarm. He had
been quite asleep . . . and yet he had remained
sitting at his desk, his eyes open. She asked him,
frightened, if there was anything wrong? "No,"
he said. "Certainly not." She asked if he wanted
anything?—if he wanted those papers taken away?
"No, nothing, I'll take them away myself," he
said abruptly. His voice was so harsh and raspy
that he forced himself to look at the girl in an
effort to smile, to soften his unpleasant manner.
And he saw, startled, that she was not a "girl"
any longer, but a mature woman. . . . He re-

membered vividly this woman as a girl, in fact as a child, and now she had a coarse, rather florid face. She was still attractive, but much heavier than he remembered. Cabral noticed also, in spite of himself, that her eyes were set rather close together.... She was embarrassed, nervous, she was asking him a question . . . and he was not listening . . . he could not hear the words, he felt that he was drowning in a mystery, a riddle. . . . There were no words to explain it or to hint at it.

When he was alone again he swept everything off his desk and wrote out this paragraph:

> Cabral, the author, died on Sunday evening, it is thought between the hours of ten and twelve. He died of no natural cause. He died of no unnatural cause either. He died. And he died in abject bitterness, cursing all the Plagiarists who sucked his life from him. His last wish was a prayer for the restoration of Hell, that such murderers should be tortured in it for eternity. His last word was Amen.

Cabral read this through carefully. He wondered if the Plagiarist who would write it might make any changes—what arrogance, what conceit, to change a single word! Cabral dared anyone to change a word. The paragraph seemed to him unassailable, perfect. Perfectly opened and perfectly closed.

To this he said aloud: "Amen."

Journey

✦

You begin your journey on so high an elevation that your destination is already in sight—a city that you have visited many times and that, moreover, is indicated on a traveler's map you have carefully folded up to take along with you. You are a lover of maps, and you have already committed this map to memory, but you bring it with you just the same.

The highway down from the mountains is broad and handsome, constructed after many years of ingenious blasting and leveling and paving. Engineers from all over the country aided in the construction of this famous highway. Its cost is so excessive that many rumors have circulated about it—you take no interest in such things, sensing that you will never learn the true cost anyway, and that this will make no difference to your journey.

After several hours on this excellent highway, where the sun shines ceaselessly and where there is a moderate amount of traffic, cars like your own at a safe distance from you, as if to assure you that there are other people in the world, you become sleepy from the monotony and wonder if perhaps there is another, less perfect road parallel to this. You discover on the map a smaller road, not exactly parallel to the highway and not as direct, but one that leads to the same city.

You turn onto this road, which winds among foothills and forests and goes through several small villages. You sense by the attitude of the villagers that traffic on this road is infrequent but nothing to draw special attention. At some curves the road shrinks, but you are fortunate enough to meet no oncoming traffic.

The road leads deep into a forest, always descending in small cramped turns. Your turning from left to right and from right to left, in a slow hypnotic passage, makes it impossible for you to look out at the forest. You discover that for some time you have not been able to see the city you

are headed for, though you know it is still somewhere ahead of you.

By mid-afternoon you are tired of this road,
though it has served you well, and you come
upon a smaller, unpaved road that evidently leads
to your city, though in a convoluted way. After
only a moment's pause you turn onto this road,
and immediately your automobile registers the
change—the chassis bounces, something begins to
vibrate, something begins to rattle. This noise is
disturbing, but after a while you forget about
it in your interest in the beautiful countryside.
Here the trees are enormous. There are no villages
or houses. For a while the dirt road runs alongside a small river, dangerously close to the river's
steep bank, and you begin to feel apprehension.
It is necessary for you to drive very slowly. At
times your speedometer registers less than five
miles an hour. You will not get to the city before
dark.

The road narrows until it is hardly more
than a lane. Grass has begun to grow in its center.
As the river twists and turns, so does the road
twist and turn, curving around hills that consist
of enormous boulders, bare of all trees and plants,
covered only in patches by a dull, brown lichen
that is unfamiliar to you. Along one stretch rocks
of varying sizes have fallen down onto the road,

so that you are forced to drive around them with great caution.

Navigating these blind turns, you tap your horn to give warning in case someone should be approaching. But it is all unnecessary, since you come upon no other travelers.

Late in the afternoon, your foot numb from its constant pressure on the accelerator, your body jolted by the constant bumps and vibrations of the car, you decide to make the rest of your journey on foot, since you must be close to your destination by now.

A faint path leads through a tumble of rocks and bushes and trees, and you follow it enthusiastically. You descend a hill, slipping a little, so that a small rockslide is released; but you are able to keep your balance. At the back of your head is the precise location of your parked car, and behind that the curving dirt road, and behind that the other road, and then the magnificent highway itself: you understand that it would be no difficult feat to make your way back to any of these roads, should you decide that going by foot is unwise. But the path, though overgrown, is through a lovely forest, and then through a meadow in which yellow flowers are blooming, and you feel no inclination to turn back.

By evening you are still in the wilderness and you wonder if perhaps you have made a mistake. You are exhausted, your body aches, your eyes are seared by the need to stare so intently at everything around you. Now that the sun has nearly set, it is getting cold; evenings here in the mountains are always chilly.

You find yourself standing at the edge of a forest, staring ahead into the dark. Is that a field ahead, or a forest of small trees? Your path has long since given way to wild grass. Clouds obscure the moon, which should give you some light by which to make your way, and you wonder if you dare continue without this light.

Suddenly you remember the map you left back in the car, but you remember it as a blank sheet of paper.

You resist telling yourself you are lost. In fact, though you are exhausted and it is almost night, you are not lost. You have begun to shiver, but it is only with cold, not with fear. You are really satisfied with yourself. You are not lost. Though you can remember your map only as a blank sheet of paper, which can tell you nothing, you are not really lost.

If you had the day to begin again, on that highway which was so wide and clear, you would not have varied your journey in any way: in this is your triumph.

Afterword

❧

In November of 1970, while I was occupied as usual with my own writing, I began to dream about and to sense, while awake, some other life, or vision, or personality. . . . Since my mind is always receptive to a multiplicity of stimuli, this did not seem to me unusual. One day I wrote a story that was strange to me, a highly abstract story set nowhere at all; I did not understand the story and in a way I felt it was not my own. I could not make sense of it and set it aside; ultimately it became "Our Lady of the Easy Death of Alferce."

The Fernandes stories came out of nowhere:

not out of an interest in Portugal (which I have never visited), or a desire to write parables to pierce through the density of existential life that I dramatize in my own writing. I much prefer the synthesis of the "existential" and the "timeless" in my own fiction; I believe that writing should re-create a world, sanctifying the real world by honoring its complexities.

If I did not concentrate deliberately on my own work, or if I allowed myself to daydream or become overly exhausted, my mind would move—it would seem to swerve or leap—into "Portugal." There seemed to be a great pressure, a series of visions, that demanded a formal, aesthetic form; I was besieged by Fernandes—story after story, some no more than sketches or paragraphs that tended to crowd out my own writing. I was able to alternate a "Fernandes" story with one of my own or with a chapter from the novel I was writing (*Wonderland*), as a kind of bargain; otherwise, Fernandes would have overwhelmed me.

The only way I could accept these stories was to think of them as a literary adventure, or a cerebral/Gothic commentary on my own writing, or as the expression of a part of my personality that had been stifled. Yet I was never able to designate myself as the author of the stories; they were all published under the name "Fernandes," and I was listed as having translated them "from the Portuguese."

Contrary to what one might believe, an experience like this—either real or imagined "possession"—is not really disturbing. Fernandes drifted into my life at a time when I was in normal health, and while his stories drained some of my energy, I was able to keep up with my own writing and my university teaching without much difficulty. It seemed that there was a harmony in what I did, without knowing what it was or why I did it; it seemed to be an almost impersonal function.

Since this experience, I have been reading voluminously in parapsychology, mysticism, the occult and related subjects, but so far I have not been able to comprehend, to my own satisfaction, what really happened. There is a considerable difference between reading about something and actually experiencing it, a lesson that intellectually oriented people must learn again and again, at times to their chagrin. My fairly skeptical and existential attitude toward life was not broad enough to deal with the phenomenon I myself experienced, and yet, at the present time, I find it difficult to accept alternative "explanations."

Repeatedly, one is brought back to the paradox that one can experience the world only through the self—through the mind—but one cannot know, really, what the "self" is. Does the brain contain the mind? Does the brain generate the mind? Is the brain a kind of organic mechanism, in each of us unique as a mechanism, through which a larger trans-human or trans-species consciousness is somehow filtered? But what would the nature of this consciousness be, and what human being could ever delude himself into imagining he might deal with it, especially in words?

Fernandes retreated when his story seemed to be complete. A kind of harmony or resolution must have been established, and the manuscript came to an end. Years later, writing this afterword, I am almost tempted to return to my earliest and most conventional diagnosis of the experience and claim it to be only "metaphorical"—the stories, the book they gradually evolved into, the afterword itself. But in truth none of it was metaphorical, any more than you and I are metaphorical.

Joyce Carol Oates

March, 1975